Where is Sophia

The tragedy in a beautiful woman's life is
what dies inside of her, while she lives.

Hanif Mike Karim

authorHOUSE®

AuthorHouse™
1663 Liberty Drive
Bloomington, IN 47403
www.authorhouse.com
Phone: 1 (800) 839-8640

Published by AuthorHouse   05/20/2016

ISBN: 978-1-5246-0913-9 (sc)
ISBN: 978-1-5246-0911-5 (hc)
ISBN: 978-1-5246-0912-2 (e)

Library of Congress Control Number: 2016908333

Print information available on the last page.

Any people depicted in stock imagery provided by Thinkstock are models, and such images are being used for illustrative purposes only. Certain stock imagery © Thinkstock.

This book is printed on acid-free paper.

Contents

This book is dedicated to my mother, Halima Bai, with deep gratitude for raising me single handedly, after passing of dad, when I was four years old. Also to my beautiful wife Nuzhat, who always believed in me, in all my endeavors.

Prologue

Two girls sit quietly in the farm field just outside the city of Douma. Last night their parents announced they would be leaving Douma, like so many others, and going to Damascus.

Damascus is the capital of Syria and lies about 16.2 km Southwest of Douma. The only city larger is Aleppo. The population there is easily over one million. The city is busy with many things to do and see. Here they would live and continue with their education.

The older sister Selma didn't like Damascus at all and vowed to herself to leave Syria and start a new life in America. It was her dream.

As was the custom, Selma had been promised in marriage to a prosperous and prominent lawyer. She protested this arrangement as she had fallen in love with a school mate, Joseph. They had agreed they would go to America together. Selma begged her mother and father to release her from the arranged marriage. They asked her to meet Mustafa and were sure this would change her mind. He was also very handsome.

The night came for Selma to meet Mustafa. While the families talked and made plans, Mustafa invited Selma for a walk. During the walk he told her that he too was opposed to the marriage as he was also in love. Selma was relieved, this way no dishonor would come to either family. Mustafa announced to both families that there would be no marriage as they both loved someone else and that there would be no further discussion. He winked at Selma and wished her well and happiness as he left with his family.

Selma and Joseph were married not long after that. They worked hard, always with the goal of moving to America. That was where they wanted to raise their family. After many years of hard work, sacrifices, and saving every possible penny, their dream came true. They were off to Los Angeles, California with their young son Danny.

Sophia, the younger sister was different. She liked to have fun and went out with her friends when she could. Like her sister, she too had an arranged marriage but to an older man, Alex, who was already a well-established doctor. They had hit it off from the moment they met, laughing and talking about so many different things. He was interesting, sophisticated and gentle, not like the other guys.

They remained in Damascus in spite of the escalating violence. And, as was the custom, they lived with his brother, wife, and mother. It was a good life and Sophia was happy. After two years Delgado, they called Alex by his last name, announced that they were pregnant. A beautiful baby girl named Mona was born.

It was a typical hot summer day in Damascus. Sophia was tending to her daughter while Delgado was doing his daily rounds at the hospital. He was busy these days, so many wounded people from the almost daily attacks by the Muslim radicals. Sophia and her family had escaped injury so far.

Sophia was preparing dinner when her phone rang. It was an official from the hospital where Delgado worked. There had been an attack. Delgado was killed. Sophia fell to her knees and cried out the pain in her heart. Her husband was her best friend, her lover, the father of their beautiful 14-year-old daughter.

Seeing her mother crying on her knees in the kitchen, Mona knew immediately what had happened. She knelt down beside her mother and tried to comfort her even though her own grief was overwhelming. Mona called her Uncle Andrew at work. He would know what to do.

The day of the funeral had come and gone. Delgado was buried in the Damascus United Congregational Church Cemetery, one of the few Christian cemeteries in Syria. Sophia, and Mona are still in shock but Andrew assures them that in time the pain will diminish.

Sophia goes through her days mechanically. Delgado's family is worried for her mental and physical health. She does not eat much or go out. She spends a lot of her time behind her closed bedroom door.

Mona is growing up quickly. The death of her father has brought the reality of the Civil War home. She longs to go and live anywhere but here. At long last she hears her mother on the telephone with her Auntie Selma in California. She has finally agreed to move to the United States.

1

Sophia's telephone rang again, for the fourth time in three days. Her older sister, Selma, kept calling from California, pressuring her to make a decision about getting out of Syria. *"You know Sophia, you've got to tell me what you want to do. You can't keep me hanging like this. I know you are under a lot of stress and it's not an easy decision to make."*

Sophia was in her early forties. She was born and raised in Syria, as a Christian in a Muslim dominant country. Her entire family's existence turned upside down three years ago when her husband was killed in a roadside bomb blast. The good doctor left behind a wife and a teenage daughter.

As traditions go in the Middle East, Dr. Alex Delgado was part of an extended family where his mother and his brother's family all lived together. So, fortunately Sophia and her daughter were not totally isolated. Although it was an arranged marriage and Dr. Delgado was considerably older, the family did not object to her pursuit of higher education. She went on to study law, although never practiced it.

Sophia's brother-in-law, Andrew, who became the head of the household after Delgado's death, was always sympathetic towards Sophia. He was aware of her deep desire to leave Syria, her dislike of the traditional entrapments and, most importantly, that she wanted to get her daughter away from there. He had never discouraged her from looking into opportunities or talking to her sister Selma in California. Sophia was appreciative of Andrew's encouragement but knew that her elderly mother-in-law would never want to hear of it. They never got along with each other from day one. The mother-in-law always complained that Sophia didn't respect her husband and Sophia felt that the old lady favored her other daughter-in-law.

Suicide bombings, sectarian killings between Shias and Sunnis, and roadside violence had become so common in Syria, that it had become a routine. There were more rumors every day that Bashar al-Assad's government would fall and ISIS would take over. That prospect was chilling for anybody, particularly non-Muslims.

Since Selma had called numerous times and left messages, Sophia knew that she must call her back before she upset her more. Selma, who was eight years older, had migrated to the United States five years earlier with her husband, Joseph, and her only son, Danny, during better times. Her husband had secured a business visa and was still working with a lawyer to establish permanent residency.

"Did I call you at a bad time, Selma?"

"No, no, it's okay, it's 7:30 already. I was about to get up anyways. I have to make breakfast for Joseph and Danny before they leave for work."

"I didn't know Danny is working with his dad."

"Oh yeah, convenience store business is hard work. Joseph can't do it by himself. Sometimes I have to go too, to help out. We have decided to put Danny's education on hold, until the business is a little more established."

"Wow, really? You, working in front of men? I can't believe it. When did you learn to speak English?"

Selma didn't answer Sophia's question but instead asked, *"So listen Sophia, what did you decide? I have to go and make breakfast. Can you call me back in a couple of hours?"*

Sophia realized that perhaps this was not a good time. *"Yes, that will be perfect. It's 9:30 p.m. right now, everybody will be asleep by then, and we can talk in peace."*

Two hours later Sophia called her sister again.

"Selma, you can't imagine how badly I want to get out of here. Things are much worse now than when you were here. Violence on the streets is rampant. Although Mona's catholic

2

school is in a safer part of the city and a special school bus takes her to school, it's still dangerous. After Alex's death my mother-in-law has become even meaner towards me than before. Thank God Andrew interferes on my behalf when she gets totally out of control, otherwise I don't know what I would do. But, even if I am able to resolve the issues with my mother-in-law, there are so many other things I am worried about in order to go there. Suppose miraculously I do succeed in getting a visa, what would I do there? I have a college degree but I have no practical experience. Where would I live with a child? See, there are a million things to think about."

Selma was listening to her calmly. *"Look Sophia, other than Mona, I am your only family now. I am like your mother. If I don't help you, who would? I am glad you told me how you feel. I will do everything within my power to get you out of there. Although, as you know, we ourselves are still trying to settle here, but you are family and I must do whatever I can."*

"You are going to make me cry, Selma."

"Please don't cry, I didn't mean to do that. I will talk to Joseph today. We have a very good lawyer, Mr. Foster. I am sure Joseph will understand and will agree with me."

"Who is this Foster?"

"He is this nice man who is helping us with the government papers. His wife recently died of cancer. He is white, but he makes us feel comfortable and understands our situation," Selma assures her.

"Well, I will let Andrew know that I have made up my mind. I will let him figure out how to handle his mother. I also have no idea how much money Alex has left for us. Andrew handles all those things."

"OK Sophia, I will have Joseph talk to Mr. Foster, and let you know what he says." The sisters agree on the plan and say goodbye to each other.

3

It was now almost noon in California. Selma usually takes lunch to her husband and Danny at the store. Sometimes after lunch she stays at the store if they need her help, otherwise she returns home. She called Joseph before leaving and he sounded busy. *"Do you want me to stay after lunch?"*

"Yes, definitely. It's real busy, maybe because it's a Friday," he replied.

During lunch Selma mentioned to him that her sister had called. Joseph already knew this, since he was still home when she had called at 7:30. Selma started to say something but he interrupted her, asking to wait until they get home since it was very busy at the store. She understood.

After closing the store at 9 p.m., they headed home. Selma warmed up the leftovers for dinner. Joseph often commented that it was the best time of the day. He could sit and enjoy a meal with his family and relax after a long day. Now he wanted to know what Selma wanted to talk to him about. He could listen without interruption now. *"So tell me, what was reason for your sister's calling so early in the morning?"*

Turning to Danny she said, *"I will tell you later."*

Danny understood that his mother didn't want him to be part of the conversation.

"Mother, I am not a child, I am 25 years old. I don't like it when you treat me this way."

"Oh no no, I didn't mean that at all. She is your only auntie. I just thought you must be tired after working all day and won't be interested in these problems."

"Well Mother, Dad has worked as much as I have, and I am much younger than he is."

"You're right. I wasn't thinking. I am sorry. Stay. Sophia told me the situation in Syria is getting really bad."

Joseph immediately jumped at that. *"So what's new? We all know that."*

"Well, let me finish. Things have gotten way worse than when we were there five years ago. Not only the violence

on the streets, the sectarian killings, the danger to the non-Muslims but also an ISIS takeover is imminent. We all know what they did to the Yazidis. Sophia is really scared. You both know, besides Mona, I am her only family. She also told me that her mother-in-law's attitude towards her has gotten much worse after Dr Delgado's death. I am like her mother. I must do whatever I can."

She looked up to see the reaction of the two men. Joseph started first. *"Look Selma, I understand you want to help your sister, but you know we are still struggling ourselves. Do you really think we are in a position to take on additional responsibilities? Our business is barely running, we have high rent to come up with every month, we have put our only child's education on hold and Mr. Foster has still not gotten us the green cards yet. I am afraid to even think what his final bill is going to be. Do you want me to go on? Oh, one more thing, as far as the problems between Sophia and her mother-in-law are concerned, your sister is not so innocent herself. I have never told you this before, but I know how she used to look at some of the men at Dr Delgado's parties. I mean, just because God has made you pretty, you don't have to flaunt it. Dr. Delgado was rich, he didn't flaunt his money, did he?"*

Joseph could sense his wife was getting a little tense with this unexpected blunt talk. *"But I understand, family is family, I will talk to Mr. Foster and let's see what he has to say."* Selma was relieved to hear that.

"What about you Danny? Are you also going to give me a hard time like your dad?"

"No Mom, I like Auntie Sophia. It would be fun to have Mona around, but do we have room to accommodate two more people? Our condo is not that big."

"Well, it will be temporary, son. When the time comes I will talk to uncle Salman's wife, she is an angel. I am sure she will get Salman's permission. We are so very fortunate to have a good landlord. We have been late so many times with our rent,

but he is always so considerate and generous. People tell me that landlords in America are really mean, and they don't let tenants be late, even for a day. Oh Joseph, I almost forgot to tell you that Sophia is going to talk to Andrew about not only moving to America, but also about her financial situation. You may not have a good impression of her, but she is a responsible person. She is fully aware that all this is going to cost a lot of money. So when you talk to Mr. Foster, please let him know that he is going to get his fee and he will not be doing any charity work. You know how lawyers can be. You remember the nightmares with our Syrian lawyers when we were trying to come here?"

"Why are you talking like that Selma? You know Mr. Foster is not like that. He has already done so much for us. Our case is not easy. Do you know how many thousands of Syrians and Iraqis are trying to flee from there and are waiting in line? He has no shortage of clients. I have given him very little money and he has gone out of his way to help me in business. It's all because he wants to help our family, so please give him some credit."

"Yes, you are right Joseph, I agree. He is a kind man, and not like other lawyers. I must say God is very kind to our family. We have come to this far away land, our own country is in shambles and we have run into people like Foster and Salman".

***

Sophia was tossing and turning in her bed, trying to figure out how and when to approach Andrew, what to say and how to say it. She was moved by her sister's kind words and the love she showed in her conversation. Before that talk with Selma, she wanted to, but didn't think she would ever be able to leave Syria. Now, it seemed that it actually might happen. She decided to wait until she found the right opportunity to talk to Andrew. The weekend was about to start so she knew he would be home.

As soon as she got a chance she told Andrew that she would like to speak to him in private. Since he was the head of the household, he commanded everybody's respect. He pointed Sophia towards the guest room. When they both got there he asked Sophia if she would like the door closed. She shyly shook her head affirmatively and he closed the door. By this time, he knew it was something serious because this was the first time they had a completely private conversation. Outside the guest room, everyone was wondering what was happening. Andrew's wife in particular had a concerned look.

"Brother Andrew, you know it's been three years since Alex has gone. I don't know what the two of us would have done without your kindness."

"Please, I don't want to hear such talk. We are family. Please don't embarrass me like this, okay?" Andrew interrupted.

"Brother Andrew, you know I have been wanting to go and live with Selma in America, if possible. The situation here is getting worse every day and I am really scared. I know it won't be easy, and thousands of people want to go, but I want to try. Selma has promised to talk to their American lawyer, who she thinks is very nice and helpful," Sophia explained.

Andrew was listening very attentively, *"Look Sophia, you know me, I have never discouraged you from doing anything you want. I admire your courage. If Selma and Joseph think that they can pull this off, then I won't stand in your way. You just let me know how I can help."*

Sophia was very happy to hear this. *"I am also worried about how mother is going to react and how much all this is going to cost."*

"Look Sophia, I never told you because this subject never came up between us, but brother Delgado has left some money for his family. I think it's around 200,000 Syrian pounds which is about 125,000 U.S dollars. This amount should be sufficient

7

to get you settled, if you can manage to get there. As far as mother is concerned, don't worry, I know how to handle her."

Sophia couldn't believe her ears. She ran to her brother-in-law to give him a hug. At exactly the same moment, the door opened and the mother-in-law came barging in. Seeing the two of them hugging, she began to scream accusations at the top of her lungs.

"I knew you were no good. I always knew that. Aren't you ashamed of yourself? What are you doing with my son?"

Sophia was stunned.

The old lady then turned towards Andrew. *"I heard you say, you know how to handle your mother. Are you so naive to fall into the trap of this no good treacherous deceiving witch? What's wrong with you? You have a family of your own."*

Out of respect, Andrew didn't shout back at his mother, although he wanted to. He tried to calm her down. Holding her hand, he led her to the sofa nearby. *"Mother, just calm down and please listen to me. Don't say such things, it's not nice. They don't suit you. You have no idea what was going on here. Let me explain everything to you. In fact, let me bring others along and let everyone know what we were talking about behind closed doors."*

He didn't have to go far. His wife, Dolly, their teenaged daughter, Deena, and Sophia's daughter, Mona, were inches away from the door dying to know what was going on. Now everyone was looking at Andrew expecting a bombshell to explode.

"What Sophia and I were talking about is this. Due to the worsening situation here in Syria, she wants to go and live with her sister Selma in America. Going there is very difficult because everyone wants to go there, but she wants to try, and Selma has promised to help. I was also assuring her that I will help because she is like my sister. She was overwhelmed with my offer to help and was thanking me when mother came in.

Mother, you shouldn't have said those mean things and I think you should apologize."

The old lady was in no mood to apologize. *"Why does she have to move there? Millions of people live here and the conditions are the same for everybody. Is she so special that she can't live here like the rest of us?"*

No one responded because they knew it would be fruitless.

Sophia's daughter was smiling. Andrew's family looked shocked. The old lady was not happy. Before leaving the room Andrew told Sophia, in front of everyone, to let him know what Selma's lawyer said. Sophia shook her head affirmatively. Mona came to her immediately after the others left and hugged her.

She was definitely enthralled. *"Mommy, are we really going to America? I can't believe it. I can't wait to tell my friends at school tomorrow."* She kept hugging and kissing her mom.

Sophia tried to curb her enthusiasm, *"Mona, please don't raise your hopes too high. We are just talking at this point. We have a long way to go. And please don't tell this to anyone yet.*

You don't know, people can get jealous and the word might spread."

***

Sophia could hardly wait to give the good news to Selma. She called her the first chance she got. *"Guess what Selma? Andrew said I can come to America and he will support me."*

"Wow, this is fantastic Sophia, how did you get him to agree so fast and what about his mother?"

"Well, his mother made a fuss as was expected, but he said to leave that up to him. God bless Andrew. He is such a wonderful man and he also told me not to worry about the money."

"Really? My goodness. Wow, this is amazing news! Look Sophia, I have also talked to Joseph and he has agreed to talk to Mr. Foster. I will keep after him and let you know in a few

days. You take care of yourself and Mona. Oh, by the way, how did she react to this whole thing?"

"Oh, Selma I can't even begin to tell you how excited she is. She has an iPhone and she's been texting all of her friends in spite of me repeatedly reminding her of how early stage this is. But you know how teenagers are.

"Okay then, Selma, I will keep my fingers crossed, and wait anxiously to see what this Foster person says. Please thank Joseph for his trouble."

"Okay Sophia, I will call you as soon as I find out."

Selma noticed Joseph's reluctance in approaching Mr. Foster about her sister, but she kept reminding him to make an appointment, which he eventually did. The earliest he could get an appointment was in two weeks.

2

The television in Andrew's mom's room was always on. This afternoon she heard a news bulletin about another roadside bomb blast. This type of news had become so common that she hardly paid much attention to it anymore. But then they said something about a school bus. Immediately she got up from bed and started screaming and shouting the names of everybody who was at home. Both women in the house, Sophia and Dolly, ran to their mother-in-law's room to see what the old lady was screaming about. Their mother-in-law was shaking with fear and anxiety. She couldn't speak, but just pointed at the television. The newsman repeated the news bulletin, that a school bus was involved in a roadside bomb blast.

The women couldn't believe their ears. They too started crying loudly, consoling and hugging each other. Both had a teenage daughter. They took the same bus and went to the same Catholic school. Dolly rushed towards the phone to call Andrew, who had already heard the news. He told her that he was headed to the police station. Trying to console his wife, he reminded her they lived in a big city and there were hundreds of schools. He also told her that the newsman kept saying that the details were still sketchy and that it was yet to be determined which school bus was involved, and how many kids were in that bus. Everyone felt so helpless. All they could do were keep their eyes glued to the TV screen.

All of a sudden the telephone bell rang. Both women sprinted to get it. Sophia got there first. It was the school superintendent. *"This is Mr. Fernandes, Madam. I am very sorry to say that some jihadi suicide bomber targeted our school bus because it was carrying Catholic children."*

Sophia dropped the phone and started screaming uncontrollably. Dolly, now picked up the phone hoping Mr.

Fernandes was still there to try to get more details. Fortunately, he was still there. He had probably experienced this reaction from the other parents that he had called. He told Dolly that there were twenty-nine kids on the bus, most of them survived although some were badly wounded. He also gave her the name and address of the hospital where the wounded were being treated.

Andrew arrived by this time and Dolly quickly told him about the call. Everybody rushed to his car to go to the hospital. The usual chaotic traffic was even worse today, sirens blowing everywhere, traffic lights mostly not working, or not being acknowledged for that matter. Andrew was doing his best to drive under these conditions while suppressing his own emotions and trying to be brave in the presence of two panicking mothers. When they were within a quarter of a mile from the hospital they were unable to go any further, the police had cordoned off the area. Andrew was somehow successful in getting the attention of a police officer. Explaining their situation to the officer, he allowed them to pass through the perimeter.

There, panicky parents were everywhere inside the hospital, some screaming in despair, others trying to calm them down. Andrew and his family were able to locate a hospital official who seemed authoritative and had access to the status of patients. For Andrew and the women, he was like a godsend. They all looked at him as if he was an angel, clinging to every word he was saying.

He took them to his office nearby and started looking at the computer screen, which supposedly had the updated status. He told them that of the twenty-nine kids, eight had been fatally wounded. The family could not speak but looked at each other with a look that said, *"Oh God, what's next?"*

The man asked for the names of the students they were looking for. The women looked at each other and Sophia pointed to Dolly to go ahead, *"Deena,"* Dolly said softly," *D E E N A."*

He looked at his list in the computer and gave Dolly a smile. She is safe. She has only minor wounds, nothing to worry about. Dolly and Andrew were so relieved they immediately looked up towards the sky and then embraced. Sophia took her hands and pressed them showing happiness for her.

Now Sophia looked at him to see if he was ready for the second name and he was. *"My daughter's name is Mona, M O N A."*

He started looking at the screen, and kept looking. Then he asked for Mona's father's name. Apparently there were two students with the same first name. Sophia said, *"Delgado, D E L G A D O."* He continued looking at the screen. Finally, he looked at Sophia with obvious distress.

"I am really sorry madam."

Sophia jumped from her chair screaming, *"No! No! No, it can't be! You're wrong! This can't be!"* She fell on the ground and started throwing up. Dolly and Andrew tried to get hold of her but she just pushed them away. She kept shouting as loudly as she could. *"Why does it always happen to me? Why? Why? Why? Where is justice?"*

Her nose was running and vomit was still apparent around the edges of her mouth. Everyone was just stunned, both by the news and the reaction of a grieving mother. Dolly again tried to embrace her and this time she succeeded as she mumbled some comforting words like, *"It must be God's wish,"* or something to that effect. As soon as Sophia heard that, she pushed Dolly away.

"God's wish, really? Why does God wish to punish me all the time? First he takes Delgado away from me, then this, and leaves me alone in this hellhole of a country where these fanatic Muslim jihadists rule."

***

13

Sophia isolated herself in her room for weeks. Everybody understood and tried not to bother her in her grieving process. She would barely talk to even her own sister. Her sister, Selma in the meantime knew that it was more urgent now to have her sister move away from Syria.

Joseph had postponed his meeting with Mr. Foster based on these new developments but Selma was pushing him to go. Fortunately, he was able to get an appointment quickly due to some cancellation.

"Hello Mr. Foster, thank you for seeing me, sorry I had to postpone my last appointment."

"That's quite all right, Joseph. Don't worry about it. It happens all the time. How are Danny and your wife? How's your business going?"

"We are all okay, Mr. Foster. But today I have come to see you not for us but somebody else."

A surprised Mr. Foster asked, "What? Who?"

"Well, it's my sister-in-law Sophia, my wife Selma's only sister. She has gone through some horrible tragedies in the last few years. First her husband was killed in a roadside bomb blast about three years ago, and now a few days ago, a suicide bomber attacked the school bus her daughter was riding in. My wife, although her sister is thousands of miles away, is going out of her mind grieving for her. I can't even imagine what her sister is going through in Syria. With her daughter gone, she is all alone in this world."

Mr. Foster was visibly shaken after what he heard. "Those bastards. So, I take it that your wife would like her sister to come and live with her? Tell me more about her. Also, will you be able to afford another person?"

"Oh, she is an educated lady. She is about forty. Her husband was a successful doctor and my wife insisted on me telling you that she will pay your full fee. She just wants to leave Syria as soon as possible".

14

Mr. Foster was listening very attentively. *"Joseph, please tell your wife that I will do everything I can for this poor woman. I think, based on her circumstances, she would be qualified for an asylum visa, which is different from how you came. You came on the business visa, which is a much longer process. I will have my secretary mail you an application. Get in touch with her in Syria, have her fill out the application, and I will see what I can do."*

Selma was happy to hear the news that Joseph had brought but now the big problem for her was to get Sophia to talk. The few times that the sisters had spoken since losing Mona, Sophia had hardly said anything at all, and had not mentioned anything about leaving Syria. Selma was afraid to bring it up worrying about the sensitivity of the timing.

A week later the application arrived. Joseph, watching his wife going through the grieving process, wanted to help. *"Do you want me to talk to her or maybe talk to Andrew?"*

"No," she said, *"let's give her more time. I will try again next week".*

After another ten days, Selma called again. Dolly picked the phone, *"Selma, I am really worried about her. She hardly comes out of her room. She doesn't want to eat and doesn't want to change clothes. We can hear her cursing at Muslims all the time. You know we don't want anybody to hear this, after all we live in Syria and it's a Muslim country. It can become more dangerous for all of us. We have tried and tried but she just wants to stay in her room, most of the time she doesn't open her door even if we knock. Selma, please try to talk to her. She really needs your help. We all need your help. Let me make another attempt. I will tell her you are on the phone."*

Dolly succeeded in getting Sophia to partially open the door. She told Sophia that her sister was calling from California. She took the handset from Dolly and closed the door again.

"How are you sweetie? We are all so worried about you."

"Selma, I feel like God has deserted me. He has abandoned me. Why should I live now? For what purpose? I just don't have any desire left to do anything. I don't even want to get out of bed. I don't know what to do. I don't know how I will live with this pain that's with me day and night. I don't know why I was born in this hellhole of a country. What kind of religion is this that tells you to kill innocent children in order to go to heaven? I will never forgive them for what they have done."

Selma was wiping her tears on the other side, while not letting her sister know, trying to comprehend how much pain her sister is going through.

"My dear, dear sister, you must be strong. I know you, you're one of the strongest people I know. Don't forget I am here. I may be far from you in distance, but in my heart and in my thoughts, you are always with me. I am praying all the time that we can be together again, so that I can share your pain. Promise me one thing, that you will never think again that you are alone. Please promise me that."

"Selma, you have no idea how badly I want to be with you, but it is going to be so hard. I don't know if I have the strength to overcome all the obstacles that I will have to face to get to you."

"Look Sophia, I was waiting for an appropriate time to tell you this. Joseph has already talked to Mr. Foster and explained everything. He is very sympathetic towards the whole situation. He has even figured out a strategy in getting you out here quickly. As I told you before, he is really a nice man. Joseph told me that when he heard about your situation, he was really moved. He even sent us an application for you right away. What do you think? Should I mail it to you? Sophia, please, you are young, you have a long life ahead of you. Always think of me when you feel alone. Call me anytime day or night. Okay, sweetie? Promise? Okay, I will send you the application tomorrow." The sisters hung up.

After receiving the application Sophia mustered enough energy to complete it. It was very painful to answer questions about her deceased family members, but she realized that it must be done. Andrew helped her with some of the questions. Everybody was relieved to see her coming out of her room more frequently.

***

Selma got Joseph to see Mr. Foster soon after she got the application back.

"Look Joseph, I have some good news. I did some checking with regard to your sister-in-law's case. I think her case can be handled on a priority basis. We can provide evidence to the immigration court that her life is in danger. Both her husband and her daughter have been killed by the fanatics. The only problem I see will be to show that they were specific targets, which I am sure that they were not. This is where we can use the religion angle. We can say to the court that the non-Muslim minorities are the imminent targets. In her case, two members of her family have already been affected. Joseph, leave it up to me. I will take care of it." He then quickly glanced over the application, to see if there were any obvious errors. He gave a long look to her picture, but didn't say anything. *"Okay, then I will call you if I need any additional information. You can let your sister-in-law know that if everything goes according to plan, she might be able to come here within four months."*

After Joseph left his office, Mr. Foster looked at Sophia's picture again, shaking his head sideways, sympathizing with the tragedy this stunningly pretty woman had to endure.

Joseph left Mr. Foster's office, anxious to get home and give Selma the good news.

When Selma heard the news, she couldn't believe her ears. She embraced Joseph tightly and wouldn't let go of him. He kept telling her that he had to go to the store where Danny was

17

handling everything by himself and then she finally did. *"Just tell me one thing before you go, how sure was Mr. Foster? Should I tell Sophia yet or not? Under no circumstances will I let her be disappointed. She is extremely fragile at the moment."*

Joseph understood, but he didn't have an answer. *"Let's just wait for a while, and not take any chances. I will call him in a couple of weeks"*.

Joseph did not call Mr. Foster's office after two weeks, in spite of every day nagging from Selma. He was being careful not to appear pushy. Then unexpectedly Mr. Foster's office called. Joseph picked up the phone and he whispered to Selma who it was. She was visibly shaking with nervousness, and got as close to the ear piece as possible while Joseph was on the phone with the lawyer.

"Joseph, we did it. Tell your sister-in-law to start making plans. She was approved much faster than I had expected. I will have my office mail you the necessary paperwork as soon as possible."

Selma was so close to the phone she heard everything. She started jumping up and down. Joseph was glad to see his wife happy after so much gloom and doom for weeks. Selma had to give Sophia the news right away no matter what time it was over there. When Sophia heard the news, it was the first time she slightly smiled after a long time.

3

Sophia's arrival at the airport was a euphoric event for all. Selma, Joseph and Sophia were all in tears, not just because of how happy they were with the sisters' reunion, but also because of what Sophia had endured. The sisters wouldn't stop hugging each other. They dropped Joseph at the shop. Sophia gave a quick hug and a kiss to her nephew Danny, and headed to her new home with Selma.

Selma had already fixed up the spare bedroom for her. Finally, the two sisters were alone face to face after so many years. Both repeatedly kept saying how hard it was to believe that this had really happened. Sophia was impressed that the condo was so roomy. Then suddenly she started weeping. Selma understood. *"You know, Mona wanted to come here so badly. I still have nightmares. It still hasn't quite sunk in yet that she's gone. I can never forgive those Muslims. First they killed Delgado and then my baby."*

"Look Sophia, there are only a few of them who have that kind of a mindset. Remember, we lived in peace when Mom and Dad were alive. We never had any trouble with them. Oh, by the way my current landlords are Muslims, so please be careful. They are a very nice couple, Zainub and Salman. In America, when you rent a place you have to sign a lease. The lease specifies how many people can live in the rental. We have a lease that allows only three, but Zainub and Salman said it was okay for you to live here. In America the renters must pay the rent on the first of the month, but they don't demand the same from us. They both think of us as our people, although they know that we are Christians. Besides this condo, they have other rental properties too. Actually they are quite well off."

Sophia was a little surprised to hear this. *"Where are they from? How did they get to become the property owners?"*

"Actually they are from Pakistan," Selma replied. *"Salman came here in the 70's and supposedly worked hard. He is really very nice, always encouraging Joseph and joking around with him. He tells Joseph he will also become a property owner soon if he keeps up the hard work. I am sure you will meet them soon."* Sophia just shrugged her shoulders as if she was not interested in meeting them or listening to anything about them.

When Joseph and Danny came home after work and everybody sat down for dinner, it was such a different environment for Sophia. She felt so much at home, and it had such a calming effect on her that tears started coming down her cheeks. This time it was different. It was the relief of being in a secure country and with her motherly sister whom she knew loved her deeply. Joseph appeared to her as if he had aged more than five years, and Danny had nicely matured and was quieter, and reserved. Her sister, she thought, had not changed one bit, same old bubbly, loving and caring.

The conversation at the dinner table mostly revolved around the happenings in Syria. Sophia told them how more and more new groups were popping up against Asad. *"It's getting more and more difficult for Asad's government to survive and simultaneously protect his supporters and the minorities,"* she explained.

"Why doesn't he just give up, and let them just kill each other?" asked Danny.

Joseph, although living in U.S., had kept track with Syrian news, interjected, *"Asad will never give up the power. He and his father before him have been ruling the country for fifty years. He doesn't know how else to live other than being a ruler. Besides, if he gives up the power, they will kill him and I don't think any other country will take him. He takes care of the generals in the army and they take care of him."*

Sophia added, *"But remember he is good for us Christians. If he leaves and those people take over, those savages will kill* all Christians, and the other minorites, rounding them up as the infidels."

Selma wanted to change the subject and asked Joseph if he or Danny would be able to take some time off so that Sophia can be shown around. *"No,"* said Joseph, *"let her rest for at least a few weeks. There is no hurry. We are extremely busy right now. I have a lot of bills to pay. Speaking of bills, that reminds me, I have to call Mr. Foster to see how much higher his bill has shot up."*

Sophia was tired and ready to go to bed. She said good night to everybody and left.

Joseph, Selma and Danny hung around at the dining table. *"My poor sister, she looks exhausted. I hope she gets some good sleep. Now remember you two, please be very careful how you deal with her, at least for the next few days. She is very fragile right now. If she says something that you don't like or don't agree with, please, just give her a pass or just ignore it. In the part of the world where she came from, politics and religion are discussed all the time. She will need to learn that in America, it's different. People here try to stay away from these subjects. I have been here over five years and I am still learning."* Both men smiled and nodded.

Joseph told Selma to drive her around the neighborhood a little bit. He also told her, when appropriate, to take her to the bank and open an account in her name. *"When the time comes Sophia will need to get Andrew to transfer her money into that account, so that Mr. Foster can get paid."* Selma gestured that she understood.

4

Two months passed since Sophia came to America. She was slowly getting used to the new life. Selma had invited some guests for dinner this evening and this would be the first time some outsiders would be introduced to Sophia. The guests were Salman and Zainub, the owners of their building. *"Doesn't Mr. Salman come around once a month to collect the rent?"* Sophia asked Selma.

"Well, they don't live close by, so we just mail them a check. This is quite common in America. Also, please don't bring up the subject of religion unless they bring it up themselves. I didn't tell you this before, but we are so far behind in rent that if it was somebody else, they would had kicked us out by now and we would have no place to live."

Sophia was shocked to hear this. *"Really? Why didn't you tell me this before? I didn't know you were in so much financial difficulty. Now I feel that I must be such a burden."*

"Oh no," Selma assured her, *"this is just temporary. You are family. You shouldn't think like that."*

Not long after this conversation Joseph and Danny came home from work. Joseph seemed to be in a good mood. He saw the table was set for the guests and commented, *"Smells really good Selma, what is it? Smells like shish kabobs that Mr. Salman likes. Did Sophia help you?"*

"Oh yes, we sisters are a team now." Selma was smiling.

The doorbell rang and Mr. Salman arrived with his wife Zainub, who was wearing a hijab. Everybody greeted each other. Selma introduced Sophia to them. Sophia was thinking, *"Oh my God, I thought I had left all these hijabi women behind in Syria, but they are here in America too."*

"I am so happy to meet you Sophia," Zainub interrupted her thoughts. *"Selma has been talking about you for five years, ever*

since I have known her. I am so glad you were able to get out of there."

Now Salman chimed in. *"Look, those ISIS savages have no business calling themselves Muslims. They are a very small minority. Their ideology is totally screwed up. That is why they are reaking such havoc and terror everywhere. I am glad this country is so vigilant, although, as you know, things have happened here too."*

Sophia didn't say anything remembering Selma's instructions. She was however pleasantly surprised to hear his views. To her, he appeared like a pleasant person.

Everybody enjoyed the meal and Selma was getting ready to make some tea according to Middle Eastern/Pakistani traditions. After tea, Salman asked Sophia if she had any plans after she settles down here in America. Sophia had not even thought about it, nor was she expecting this question. *"Well, I don't know. I would like to do something, but don't know what".*

Selma jumped in. *"You know she's a college graduate and was one of the top students in her class."* Sophia gestured towards her sister to keep quiet, as if she was embarrassing her.

Salman was showing interest in knowing more. *"You see, it's important to keep yourself busy. Obviously you are not going to sit at home all day not doing anything, you will get bored. Look, we like Joseph, Selma and Danny. We don't think of them as tenants, they are more than that. So please let us know if there is anything we can do to make the transition to your new life smoother."*

Joseph and Selma were visibly grateful for his gestures, and were thanking him profusely. Salman and Zainub thanked everybody for their hospitality and left.

After they left everybody was looking at Sophia to see her reaction since she had been so skeptical of them. Sophia was quite obviously impressed by their sincerity and genuineness *"Wow, he was really nice,"* she commented.

Selma told her, *"Zainub is equally nice although she doesn't talk much."*

***

Another month had passed by and Sophia was learning about America much faster than the average new comer. She had familiarized herself with the neighborhood and she had even gotten a driver's permit. She also went to Joseph's store sometimes, to help out and had learned how to deposit/ withdraw checks at a bank. Andrew had already transferred her money into her account as he had promised. Selma was very pleased with how things were turning out for her sister and how quickly she was acclimatizing with the changes. Sophia herself, in her quiet moments, couldn't believe how her life had changed in a few short months. Joseph was appreciative of an additional helping hand and to see how happy his wife was. His business had also picked up a little. Danny had always enjoyed his auntie's company and he was now old enough to understand what she had gone through.

When they were alone, Joseph often discussed finances with Selma, among other things. *"So what do you think, should we tell Sophia that we haven't paid Mr. Foster yet? After all it's been months and he got her here so quickly. Just because he's been nice and not pushing us, that doesn't mean we should take advantage of that. Yes?"*

Selma agreed. *"I am sure she will have no problem paying him his fees. I will talk to her. Can you call him tomorrow and find out how much it is? And, while you are at it, see if he will tell us how much we owe him in our own case."*

The phone rang, and when Selma picked up, it was Salman on the line. *"How are you? How's the family?*

"Fine, Brother Salman. How are you and Sister Zainub?"

"Listen Selma, the reason I called is this. You know I have a few properties right? Well, I have a guy who manages those properties. He works from an office that is not far from where you live. He could use some help and I was wondering if your sister would be interested in working at that office? This way she can be productive, learn how things work in America and start to become more independent. What do you think? Talk to her and Joseph and let me know. Oh, by the way, there are buses that go by near the office, so she doesn't have to worry about needing a car."

"Oh thank you, Brother Salman, you are very kind. I will call you back soon."

Selma called Joseph right away. He thought it was a great opportunity. Then she talked to Sophia, who was apprehensive at first, but then decided it would probably be good for her. She also thought about the money that she could give to Selma to help cover her living expenses. Selma told Sophia that she would give her ride for the first few days, but then she can start taking the bus.

Salman greeted the two sisters at the office on the first day. "Hello ladies, how are you two doing? Welcome to my office. Let me introduce you to my office manager. This is Jose Lopez. Jose has been running this office for the last several years. I personally don't come here every day, but Jose does. He takes care of eight properties for us. That keeps him very busy. Jose, this is Selma who you already know, and her sister Sophia. Sophia is going to be helping you, take good care of her, she is new in America. Teach her slowly everything you know about property management."

Jose nodded, and shook hands with them. "Welcome. Please don't worry. A few years ago I didn't know anything either. Boss Salman taught me everything."

Salman smiled proudly then told them he had to go to a meeting and then left.

Selma also left after a few minutes, letting Sophia know that She would pick her up later in the evening.

Sophia was now alone with Jose. All of a sudden it dawned on her that she is all by herself with a man who is a stranger. She was not quite used to this kind of scenario, coming from the Middle East.

Jose was a heavy set, mustached, Hispanic man in his thirties. Noticing her obvious nervousness, he tried to make her comfortable by telling her about himself.

"Look Sophia, I wasn't born in this country either, and eleven years ago, when I came here from Mexico, I was totally lost myself. I didn't have a job and having married young, I had three young daughters and a wife to support. But things turned around. They always do. I did menial jobs, learned English, went to school at night and did what I had to do. So don't worry, I will teach you everything. You have your sister in this country, you can speak English, and you're lucky to get a job so quickly, jobs are very hard to find these days".

Sophia listened to Jose's story carefully. Now it was her turn to speak, *"Jose, please don't tell me again that I am lucky."* Jose was a little taken aback when he heard this, particularly since these were the first words coming from her mouth. She went on and told him her story. Although he had come from a country that was also known for atrocities and violence, by the time she was done, Jose had teary eyes.

Sharing their personal stories helped them to understand each other. Now it was time to go to work. Anticipating a new person joining him in the office, Jose had already set up a desk for her. Jose elaborated first on the basics of what Salman expected of them as a team, and then showed her how and what she could do to help him out. He told her that Salman had specifically instructed him not to send her out to the tenants for rent collections, problem resolutions, and other types of things. That was supposed to be taken care of by Jose, himself. Jose noticed that Sophia was picking things up fast, in spite of everything being new to her.

***

Within six months Sophia had become quite good at her job. Salman had even given her a nice salary increase which she thought was very generous of him. She had also noticed that Salman had started to come to the office more frequently. Many times when Jose was out they would be alone. He always seemed to know what Jose was doing and stayed in constant touch with him.

Sometimes he would sit on a chair next to her desk for a casual chitchat, other times he would ask her to join him for a chat in his office. At times he would take Jose and her out for lunch and, since he was the boss, on those days there was no hurry to return to work. She always enjoyed the long relaxed lunches.

Today was different, he asked her to go for lunch, and it was just the two of them. Jose was out. Thai food was her favorite and that's where he said they were going. At first it seemed a little awkward, but she had become quite comfortable with him by now. She was surprised to learn that in spite of him being a Muslim, he didn't mind having a drink now and then. Since this was the first time they were in a restaurant alone, he somewhat opened up to her. He told her how he felt alone in spite of being a married man.

"My wife and I have very little in common. She has no interest in anything other than religious activities and shopping. I keep telling her to take some classes, learn some new things but she won't. You know she can't even go on the internet or send a text message and she is a college graduate. Oh well. So tell me about yourself. You have been here almost a year now, right? How do you like it here so far? Are you satisfied with the pace of your settling down? Joseph tells me his business has picked up. He is a hard worker, very nice guy. I knew he would do well here."

27

"Yeah, I have been slowly getting comfortable in this country. My sister has been helping me a lot, and also I have to thank you for being so nice to me."

"So have you made new friends, met new people? Jose tells me you have become quite good at going on line and visiting different web sites and stuff."

"Yes, we do have a good size Syrian community here and we do get together sometimes. It's nice. Should we go back to the office? Jose must be back by now."

Jose was back. He tried not to act surprised that the boss took her for lunch alone. After a few minutes Salman left.

"How was lunch?" Jose asked.

"Oh it was fine."

"You know Sophia, it's none of my business, but I must tell you to be careful. The only reason I am saying this is because I care about you. You know he is our boss and everything, but he is a married man and I have seen him with other women."

"Really?" Sophia was surprised.

"Yeah. I think he doesn't care much about his wife because he thinks she is too conservative and doesn't like to have fun, like him. Please don't let him know that I said this. I don't want to lose my job."

"Oh no, Jose don't worry, you have done so much for me. I don't know how will I ever repay you. But thanks for letting me know."

Salman was coming to the office and taking Sophia to lunch more frequently. Sophia noticed that he was less inhibited and they exchanged jokes and laughed more. Although he was much older, she didn't mind because he made her comfortable. She liked the fact that he was very unpretentious and never acted like a boss with her or Jose. The only time he made her feel uncomfortable was when he went on and on about how pretty she was. Sophia would tell everything to Selma when she got home, who would get a kick out of it.

5

Sophia had not yet received the final U.S. residency papers and was anxious to receive her green card. Joseph had enquired about the status of the green card a few times but he was always told to call back later. Now that Sophia was used to calling Salman's tenants, she didn't hesitate calling Mr. Foster's office herself. She was told that her green card had just arrived from the immigration office and can be picked up the next day. Sophia had learned to use a GPS device, and she decided to take a day off and go to pick up the green card on her own. She had heard so many nice things from Selma about Mr. Foster and wanted to thank him personally.

"I am here to see Mr. Foster," she said to the office secretary. The secretary had her take a seat on the couch while she went to let Mr. Foster know she was waiting. After she waited for about half an hour, he came out to greet her. He escorted her to his office. Sophia immediately noted that Mr. Foster's office was enormous. They sat at a large conference table, he on one side and she on the other.

"I am so pleased to finally meet you. How do you like United States? Sorry it took so long to get your green card. At least we were able to get you the asylum visa quickly, that's what was important, right? So how are you doing?" Foster couldn't keep his eyes off the beautiful woman in front of him.

"Oh, I am fine sir. I wanted to thank you for helping me. Joseph told me how difficult it is, because so many people want to come here and you got me here so fast. I couldn't believe it at first. You made my dream come true."

"Oh please, I was just doing my job. Besides, I want you to know that contrary to what you hear about United States, we are a compassionate country. Based on the horrendous circumstances you were living under, I knew that you would

get the papers quickly. Look, you may not like what I have to say, but I think they are savages. They are the worst people on this planet. I would carpet bomb them and wipe them out if it was up to me."

Sophia was shocked to hear those views from him, mostly because they were her own views, and she was hearing them from someone else. *"Mr. Foster I cannot tell you how much I hate them for what they have done to me. What did I do to them? They do it all in the name of religion."*

Mr. Foster kept shaking his head, *"Religion? What religion? Nobody in his right mind can think that any religion can tell you to do such horrific things".*

Mr. Foster was completely enthralled with this beautiful woman. It was late morning and almost lunch time. He took the opportunity to ask if she would like to have lunch with him. She readily agreed. Mr. Foster called his secretary to ask when his next appointment was. She advised him he didn't have any appointment for the next two hours.

Sophia thought Mr. Foster had not only played an instrumental role in changing her life, but was also very charming and understanding. She was very impressed with how this white American man could be so successful in life, yet be so humble and down to earth. Over lunch he told her that his wife had passed away two years ago due to cancer. Sophia had already heard this from Selma. Mr. Foster was very attentive and paid may compliments to Sophia during their meal. She sensed that Mr. Foster found her to be attractive. *"So, I know that you didn't practice law, but how many years of college do you have under your belt? Did you take an exam over there at the end, like we are expected over here?"*

"Well I did four years, and yes, I did pass the exam. I was married when I went to college. My in-laws would not allow me to work. I was already way beyond what most women normally do in that culture. My husband had modern ideas as compared

to the general public and that's why I was allowed to go to college in the first place."

Mr. Foster asked if she had ever looked into the American law and compared it with what they had over there. She had not and told him as much.

"If given a chance, would you consider going back to school?"

"Well, I have never thought about it. I am sure it is probably very expensive. I don't think I would be able to afford it".

"Yeah, but affordability is not everything. It would take a lot of hard work, focus and perseverance. Do you have that in you? I know you are relatively new here and probably still learning the culture."

"You see, I have a full time job, I would like to work there for a while, and after saving some money, I will think about it."

"Oh really, so tell me about your job, what do you do?"

"Well, I work in an office. My sister's landlord owns a lot of different properties. He has one person who manages all his properties. I am the manager's assistant."

"Oh, that sounds interesting. Do you like it?"

"Yeah, I like it. My manager, Jose, is a very nice man. I have learned a lot from him."

"What about Jose's boss? Is he nice too?"

"Yeah, he's nice too. He is from Pakistan, but he is not a strict Muslim".

Mr. Foster' eyebrows went up when he heard that. "How can you tell whether someone is a practicing Muslim or not? Look I have dealt with a lot of Pakistanis. Most of them are crooks. If I had to bet, I would say that this fellow Jose is from Mexico, doesn't have a green card, and that Pakistani guy is exploiting him by giving him low wages and so on."

"How did he know he was from Mexico?" She was really surprised and impressed, not knowing that the name Jose was very common in Mexico.

31

"All I can tell you is that you better be careful with that Pakistani guy. I wouldn't trust him. He may be nice outwardly, but those guys usually have some ulterior motives."

Sophia, still new to the country, didn't even realize how racist and prejudicial those remarks were, particularly coming from an officer of the court. His comments only refreshed her angry feelings towards Muslims. In her mind she now had even deeper respect and admiration for Mr. Foster. She thought of him as somebody who was not only on her side, but completely understood her feelings and shared her thoughts and ideas.

"Look Sophia, if you decide to go back to school, I can help you. Of course it is hard work, but it will be easier for you than most other people, because you already know the basics of law. Once you graduate you can work with me. You can earn in a month here, what that Pakistani guy probably pays you in a year."

Sophia was quite taken aback by this generous offer. She couldn't believe what she was hearing. *"Oh, Mr. Foster, you are so kind. Let me talk to my sister and I will let you know."*

"Oh, yes, yes, take your time. I understand it's not an easy decision to make."

Selma was waiting anxiously for Sophia to return from Mr. Foster's office. Selma wanted to see her reaction after meeting him for the first time. Sophia had mentioned to Selma several times how her life had changed, how nice people had been to her and Mr. Foster was a big part. Sophia also knew that Selma would want to know what she thought of Foster, after actually meeting him.

"Oh, Selma I can't begin to tell you how unbelievably nice Mr. Foster is. Not only was he charming and good at making me feel comfortable, he is also so humble and down to earth. He took me for a long lunch, and took so much interest in how I was doing in America. He even offered to help if I wanted to go back to school and get a law license. Joseph must have told

him that I went to college in Syria. Selma, I don't know what to do. I have been here more than a year. I should have met him sooner. He is so wonderful."

"Okay, Okay, take it easy, don't get carried away. Come on, you know, men always want to help beautiful women. He probably couldn't resist saying those things. After all, he is a single man although he is a lot older than you."

Sophia started to blush. *"Look Selma, first of all I am not so beautiful and then he is probably the same age as Delgado."*

"Oh, so you do think of him that way, I see." Both sisters were laughing.

Soon after that Joseph and Danny were back from work.

Joseph asked, *"What's going on? What's so funny? Aren't you going to share with us?"*

Selma looked at Sophia. *"Should I tell him?"*

"Go ahead, I don't care."

"Okay, so my little sister went and saw Mr. Foster today, and seems to be quite impressed by him." She told Joseph with a wink.

"Oh my goodness, really Sophia? Is it one sided or two sided?"

"Joseph, Selma is just acting a little crazy these days. Nothing happened, he was probably just trying to be nice."

"Not just a little nice, he wanted her to finish her schooling and join him in his office," Selma boasted.

"But did you tell him that you already have a full time job? How are you going to find time? And it's probably very expensive."

"Yeah, I told him all that. He asked me to think about it."

The next day when Sophia went to work, Salman wasn't there, but Jose was.

"How was your day off Sophia? Did you enjoy yourself?

"Yes I did. Thanks. Jose, can I ask you a question? It's kind of personal. You know I have told you everything about myself. In fact, we've both told each other everything, right?"

33

Jose was a little taken aback. *"Sure Sophia, what is it?"*

"Jose, are you a citizen here or is Salman helping you in some way?"

Now Jose was stunned. He didn't expect this at all. *"Sophia, why would you ask me such a question?"*

"Well, I thought we had that kind of friendship where we don't hide anything from each other. If you don't want to tell me it's okay." Sophia's suspicion grew stronger.

"Okay, Okay, I will tell you. But remember, outside my family, only you and Mr. Salman know this. No, I don't have the papers. It is almost impossible to get an office job without a green card but Mr. Salman hired me anyway. Maybe he pays me less, I don't know, but I am happy to have this job."

Sophia once again thought about Mr. Foster, realizing that he had been right again.

6

Not much had changed in the next six months. Sophia had visited Mr. Foster twice since the initial meeting. Both times he took her out for lunch and showed interest in how things were going in her life. He was also upfront about his personal life, and didn't hesitate to tell her he missed female company. Sophia didn't discourage him and wanted to leave the door open for the time being. He even gave her his private cell phone number. *"Call me if you ever need anything".*

Salman in the meantime was still coming around frequently and taking Sophia for lunch at every opportunity. As usual, he would complain about his wife and Sophia would listen. Over time, they had also become much more familiar with each other, occasionally giving friendly hugs, and other casual contact. One particular day, when Jose was not in, Sophia noticed Mr. Salman was in an unusually good mood when he asked her to lunch.

"Where would you like to go for lunch today Sophia?"

She mentioned the Thai place she liked.

"Oh I like that place too. Let's go a little early today, that place gets crowded at lunch time."

Salman ordered a bottle of white wine instead of his usual beer today and Sophia wondered why. *"Is it a special occasion today?"*

"No, I am just happy to be having lunch with such a pretty lady."

Sophia was accustomed to being complimented on her looks by now. They shared the wine which made her feel a little tipsy. She was not really concerned as she was with the boss and really didn't think too much about it. On their way back to the office, she was thinking about how nice it was to be in

America. She had a job. She was close to her sister and she felt secure here as compared to Syria.

Back in the office Salman commented, *"I really shouldn't be driving after drinking. I could get into big trouble if I get stopped by a cop. Let's sit here for a while,"* he suggested pointing to the couch meant for office visitors. *"Man, I am really full. I think ate too much. How about you, did you enjoy the lunch?"*

"Oh yeah," Sophia said, *"it was great, thanks so much."*

"I tell you what, let's forget about work for a while." After having said that, he got up and locked the outside door. Sophia gave him a surprised look when he came back and sat next to her.

"Ok, the office is closed for business today," he said. Sophia just smiled and didn't say anything, wondering what he was up to. In the almost two years she'd worked for him he had never touched her inappropriately.

"So Sophia, you like working here, yes?"

"Of course. You know I do Mr. Salman. Why do you ask?"

"Oh, don't call me Mr. Salman. Just call me Salman. You can call me Mr. in front of Jose, but not when we are alone. I don't like these formalities between us. You know Sophia, I like you a lot right?" he said as he started inching towards her.

Sophia was confused, yet she didn't resist. It had been a long time since any man had actually tried to come close to her. She was used to getting compliments, but sometimes wondered what good those compliments were for, when nobody ever came near her? Here was this nice man, although older, who had been so nice to her and her family, trying to get close to her.

"But you are married, Salman. What will happen if the Mrs. finds out?" Although it was a serious question, Sophia asked with a smile on her face.

Her smile gave Salman enough encouragement. *"Oh, she will never find out. Who is going to tell her?"* Saying that, he put his arm around her. At first he softly kissed her on her neck, then on her forehead and then planted a big kiss on her lips.

Sophia was dazed, she didn't know what was going on. She was in a state of confusion but she didn't stop him. He was more encouraged when there was no resistance. *"Oh Sophia, you are so beautiful. I wanted you the first time I laid my eyes on you."* By now he was unzipping her blouse, and still there was no resistance.

The couch was not wide enough for two people to lie down side by side, so they decided to lie down on the carpet. Sophia was more confused after they were finished. So many different thoughts were going through her head. Some of the events replayed in her head over and over again. His words, *"I wanted you the first time I laid my eyes on you, "*made her wonder if that meant he'd been planning this for a long time and just waiting for the right opportunity? She even saw an open package of condoms nearby. Did that mean he was planning this all along? Another thought kept coming to her, was what Mr. Foster said about him, "Don't trust those Pakistani guys. They may be nice from outside, but they usually have ulterior motives." Was Mr. Foster right again? He had not been wrong about anything so far. The thought that bothered her most was, did I let this Muslim guy take advantage of me? Haven't these Muslims caused enough havoc and destruction in my life? This last thought was just too much for her to bear.

In the meantime, Salman was lying next to her, happy as could be. He had no idea what kind of commotion was going on in the person's head lying next to him.

"Everything okay? What are you thinking?" Salman asked her with a soft kiss on her cheek, *"you have been so quiet."*

"I have to go. I'm not feeling well."

"Are you sure? It's only three o'clock."

"Yes, I must go now. I don't feel good."

She left soon afterwards.

Salman was a little surprised, but chalked it up to some emotional problem she might be having.

On her way home Sophia became angrier and confused. It got to the point that she stopped her car on the side of the road and called Mr. Foster.

"Mr. Foster, you were right about Salman." He could sense her heavy breathing and nervousness.

"Calm down Sophia, who is Salman? And are you okay?"

"Salman is that Pakistani guy I told you about. I work with him in his office. He is also my sister's landlord."

"Oh now I remember. What happened, what did he do?"

"You warned me about him, but I didn't listen."

"So what did he do? Did he hurt you?"

"Worse. He took me for lunch. Made me drink wine and took advantage of me in his office."

"Oh no! That son of a bitch! When did this happen?"

"About an hour ago."

"Where are you right now? Can you come to my office right away?"

"I have to go home, clean up and change before I can come."

"No, no, no. Listen to me carefully. What I am about to tell you is very important. Do not change and do not clean up. Just come to my office straight from where you are. Okay?

"But I don't want you to see me like this. I feel dirty."

"Sophia please don't worry about how you look right now, just do as I tell you."

After talking with Sophia, Mr. Foster cleared his calendar for the rest of the afternoon and discussed the situation with a criminal lawyer, David Bernstein.

Sophia was obviously distraught and exhausted when she got there. Mr. Foster gave her a hug and tried to calm her down. She started crying, mumbling that she should had listened to him. A few minutes after she arrived, he picked up the phone but did not tell her who he was calling. Sophia only heard his end of the call.

"My name is John Foster, I am an attorney, and I want to report a crime. The victim's name is Sophia Delgado. She was raped by her boss after getting her drunk during work hours." He went on to give them his office address on the phone.

When he was finished with the call he took her to a nearby hospital, where they checked her thoroughly as well as asked her many questions, some were very embarrassing. Foster saw how exhausted she was after her day's ordeal but the day wasn't over yet. He still had to brief her in terms of what to expect next. Sophia was tired but went with Foster to a nearby coffee shop to listen to what would come next.

"Look I know you have gone through a lot today, but unfortunately all victims have to go through this process, to gather evidence. You have studied law, you already know why we are doing all this. Another thing, unfortunately it is not over yet. I got a call from my office while you were in the examination room. A couple of police investigators are waiting to get a statement from you.

You think you can handle them?"

"All this is happening too fast. My head is spinning. My sister doesn't even know anything yet. I don't know how she will take all this. What will Joseph say? Salman and his wife are family friends. My sister owes them a lot of money."

"Well, Salman shouldn't have done what he did. When you commit a crime there are consequences you must face".

"But Mr. Foster, I am a grown woman. What if they ask me why I went with him in the first place? After all he did not force me to drink."

"First of all, being an authoritative figure and your boss, he shouldn't be drinking during work hours with his subordinate. Second, I don't think they will ask you those kinds of judgmental questions. Besides, I will be there next to you and I can intervene if they get out of line.

"Okay let's go. Let's not make them wait too long, they might get pissed."

As soon as they entered the car to go back to Mr. Foster's office, Sophia's phone rang. It was Selma wondering where she was.

"Where are you Sophia, are you okay? I was getting worried."

"I am okay Selma, don't worry. I had to see Mr. Foster about something. I will tell you about it when I come home."

Detective Steffan and detective Murphy were waiting in the office lobby.

"I am John Foster and this is my client Sophia Delgado. Sorry you guys had to wait, I had to take her to the hospital. I hope you understand".

"Oh sure, we understand, no worries," Detective Steffan said.

"So let's go inside and we can talk," suggested Foster.

All four of them entered the office. Detective Steffan, who seemed to be the lead person, asked Murphy to start. Murphy took out a tape recorder from his pocket and pushed the record button.

"So Miss Delgado, just for the record, you are being recorded and your representing attorney is present."

"What is your full name?"

"Sophia Delgado."

"Are you a citizen of United States?"

Sophia looked at Mr. Foster.

"She has a permanent residency status. Her citizenship paperwork is in process."

"What is the name of the person who committed the crime, and how do you know him"?

"His name is Mr. Salman, and he is my boss."

"What kind of business is it"?

The interview went on for two hours.

In the meantime, Selma and Joseph were worried after not getting any responses to their calls. They drove to Mr. Foster's office and waited in the office lobby. The sisters hugged when

Sophia came out. Selma was relieved to see her sister safe and sound. Selma and Joseph were anxious to know what was going on. Both looked at Mr. Foster for some answers.

"Look, if you are worried about her immigration status, don't be, nothing has changed and she is fine. Take her home and let her rest for a while. She has been through some traumatic experiences today. She will tell you when she is ready."

Sophia went straight to bed after taking a shower. The next day she did not go to work nor did she call in. It was unusual for her not to let Jose know that she wasn't coming in. Jose, worried, called her. She didn't answer. She finally went downstairs around ten. Selma knew there was something horribly wrong but waited for Sophia to start the conversation about yesterday's events.

Having spent several hours with Foster the previous evening, who repeatedly assured her it was all Salman's fault, Sophia was convinced that the whole thing happened because of Salman, and she was definitely a victim. So when she started telling Selma what had happened, she started immediately by saying, *"That Pakistani friend of ours took away my dignity. He wined me, dined me and then took advantage of me."*

Selma couldn't believe her ears, *"What? No, No. Oh my God. My poor sister."* She kept hugging Sophia and wouldn't let go. *"This is unbelievable. I thought he was such a gentleman; he has always been so nice to us. What are you going to do? What about your job? What if Zainub finds out?"*

"Well, Mr. Foster had warned me about him. I should have listened. So when this happened, I called him, because I know he understands me and will tell me what's the right thing to do. When I went to see him he got me medically checked out and also made a police report."

The word police freaked Selma out even more. *"Oh my God, even the police are involved?"* Now she was really panicking. She immediately called Joseph.

"You won't believe what Salman did to Sophia yesterday. He got her drunk and took advantage of her." Selma was repeating what Sophia told her.

"Wait, wait wait. How do you know what happened? You are just repeating what Sophia told you, right?

"Of course. I know my sister; she is not going to lie to me." Selma was upset at what he was insinuating, and for doubting her sister.

Joseph didn't want to argue on the phone. *"Look just calm down. We will talk when I get home."*

"But Mr. Foster reported this to the police," Selma blurted out.

"Police? Oh no. I better come home right away." He hung up the phone.

***

Jose was alone in the office. It was different with Sophia not being around. Some time around mid-morning there was a knock on the door and a couple of policemen entered asking if Mr. Salman was there. Jose told them he wasn't, and they asked for his home address. Jose gave it to them. As soon as the policemen left he called Salman to let him know about their visit and that he had been obliged to provide them with his home address.

"Mr. Salman, there were some cops, who came to the office looking for you. They made me give them your home address."

Sounding surprised Salman asked Jose, *"What did they want? Did they say they were going to my house?"*

"I think so. And by the way, I am by myself today."

"What do you mean, where is Sophia?"

"She didn't come to work today, and she didn't call. When I called her, she didn't pick up her phone."

Salman started wondering what was going on. She went home in a hurry yesterday, today she didn't go to work, she didn't call and wasn't picking up her phone. He called Sophia himself. She didn't pick up. He called Selma's house, Selma picked up, *"Hello Selma, how are you?"*

"Hi."

"Is Sophia all right? She didn't come to the office."

"She is not feeling well."

Salman could sense the change in Selma's tone toward him and now he was starting to panic. *"Can I speak with her?"*

"She doesn't want to speak with you."

"Look, we have been family friends for a long time Selma, and I have been good to your family, and this is how you to treat me?" He abruptly hung up. Now he knew why the police were looking for him. He knew he had to get out of the house before they arrived and arrested him.

Joseph came home in a hurry, leaving Danny at the store. Sophia had overheard his earlier conversation on the phone with Selma. Both sisters dreaded talking to Joseph and knew it was not going to be easy.

"Sophia, look you are my wife's little sister and she is like a mother figure to you, that means I'm like a father figure. So please tell me exactly what happened. I will tell you upfront, unlike your sister, I am not willing to put the entire blame on him unless you can convince me otherwise."

Selma intervened, *"I think he had designs on her from the very beginning, that's why he was being nice to her and gave her the job."*

"Oh really? He was nice to us much earlier than Sophia's getting here. Maybe he had designs on you too Selma," Joseph said sarcastically. *"Now let Sophia talk. I want to know from her, what actually happened."*

Sophia knew fully well that Joseph was not going to let her get away without telling him everything. She also knew through Selma that Joseph had made some comments about

43

her unfaithfulness, and suspected that Delgado may not be the only man she had slept with.

"This is what happened," Sophia began. *"As you know, he has many properties, and he had only one person, Jose, to take care of everything. Jose had to go collect rent from the tenants, do paperwork, answer phones, deposits and withdrawals from the bank, everything. So Jose trained me to do the work inside the office while he did the outside work. Before I started working there, Jose told me that Salman hardly ever went to the office."*

"What do you mean?" Joseph interjected, *"How can you run a business without going to the office?"*

"Salman kept in constant touch with Jose, and completely trusted him. Jose is a very nice family man. He is very honest and hardworking. Salman knows Jose will never betray him, because he knows some of Jose's secrets. So when I started working there, Salman started to come to the office more frequently. He would come around lunch time, and all three of us would go for lunch. Occasionally he would have a drink or two himself but Jose and I never had any. Lately, he was coming in more frequently and he was coming only when Jose wasn't there so that I could go to lunch with him alone."

Joseph interjected again, *"So why did you go with him if you knew his game? Why couldn't you say no? Did you give him the impression that you were enjoying the lunches too?"*

Sophia had a puzzled look on her face. Selma came to her rescue, *"Joseph, how can she say no? That's not nice and he was her boss."*

Joseph was not about to buy that. *"Look, I have been in this country for seven years, no employer can ask his subordinate to do anything they don't want to do. But let Sophia finish. So tell us what happened yesterday."*

"Jose had a day off, obviously Salman knew that. We went for lunch early. I think he had planned everything because he looked very happy. At lunch he ordered a bottle of wine which he never did before. I remember he kept pouring for me and

kept my glass full. We had a long lunch and when we got back to the office, I was too dizzy and blacked out. When I woke up he was on top of me and I realized what had happened. I also saw a package of condoms nearby. I was very confused and got out of there quickly. He knew I was angry and didn't even try to stop me".

"On my way home I decided to call Mr. Foster. He told me to come straight to his office, without changing clothes or taking a shower. That's what I did, because I trust him. When I got to his office, he had already contacted the police. He also took me to a nearby hospital to get me checked out and to record the evidence. When we came back from the hospital, the police investigators asked me questions for more than two hours. I told them everything that I am telling you now. When we came out of the office after the interrogation, you two were waiting for me in the lobby."

Selma looked at Joseph, "So, you heard everything, are you satisfied now?"

Joseph just kept shaking his head sideways and mumbling, "What a mess, what a mess. God help us."

"Oh I almost forgot to tell you," Selma remembered, "Salman called. He asked about Sophia's not going to work, and then wanted to talk to her, but she refused. Then he mumbled something about how much he has done for us, blah blah blah."

Joseph, even after hearing the whole thing was still skeptical. "Sophia, you must know that Salman has done a lot for this family. I still owe him several thousand dollars. He helped me in business. His wife is a decent human being. I have heard Selma refer to her several times as an angel. We cannot ignore all that."

Selma interjected, "But what about what he did to Sophia?"

"Look, I admit that Salman probably likes her, but I also believe that he must have gotten the impression that she liked him too. These are two grown-up adults we are talking about."

"How can you say that? He's so old?" Selma protested.

"As far as being old is concerned, Sophia was married to Dr. Delgado, who was an older man. She likes Mr. Foster; he's about the same age as Salman isn't he?"

"But I never thought of Salman that way. I can never think about a Muslim that way." Sophia said angrily.

"Oh, so now the truth comes out. What has religion got to do with this?"

"It has everything to do with this. Don't you understand? They have destroyed everything in my life. I despise them with every fiber in my body." Sophia was livid.

"You are mixing the two things up. One is religion, and the other is some fanatics who, in their ignorance and jihadi mentality, are hell bent on destroying everything," Joseph argued.

"Joseph, it is easy for you to say all these things. I wonder if you would feel this way if your spouse and your only child had been taken away," Sophia countered.

"Look, Sophia I am sorry. I didn't mean to refresh the sufferings you have gone through, but please remember we all suffered. We had to leave our country, our roots of many generations. Selma and I also left everything we had. At this age, I had to start all over again and I am still struggling. Danny didn't even finish his education. I still think that you shouldn't have gotten the police involved. Look, don't forget we are still newcomers in this country. We don't want to be looked at as trouble makers. Had you come home instead of going to Mr. Foster, I believe we could have prevented the police getting involved. Foster is an American, they think differently than we do. We could have come to some kind of resolution amongst ourselves. Don't forget Foster is a lawyer, lawyers like conflicts, that's how they make a living."

Selma interrupted, *"What happened to all the praises you use to heap on Mr. Foster? As to how great he was, and how he wants to help our family and all that?*

"I still think he has helped us a lot and I will always be grateful, but in this case, I think he pulled the trigger too quickly. Think about it, he knew that Sophia was working in Salman's office, and Foster is himself interested in her. What better way than to get your competition involved with police to get him out of your way. Haven't you heard of killing two birds with one stone?"

Both Sophia and Selma were surprised to hear Joseph's thinking. In some ways it made sense and sounded logical, yet neither one of them was willing to admit that Foster could be so cynical.

7

Salman wasted no time after he hung up the phone with Selma. The first thing he did was to leave the house before the police got there. He deliberately kept his wife in the dark to not cause any alarm. He knew he had to find a good lawyer quickly. He didn't know any criminal lawyers so he called his tax lawyer, who was also his golf buddy, to get a recommendation. After listening to the gist of his case, his friend suggested that he should hire a woman attorney, who he thought were better at handling these types of cases. He also recommended a specific attorney, Nancy Sweeney.

Nancy Sweeney was a partner in a large law firm. She was able to reshuffle her schedule to accommodate Salman whose case needed immediate attention. She listened to everything that Salman had to say.

"It's a very serious matter Mr. Salman. Right now you could be considered a fugitive, since your subordinate Jose had already told you that the police wanted to question you. You chose to dodge them. The judges don't look at these actions kindly. So, the first thing you need to do is to go to the local police station voluntarily, and make yourself available for questioning. If they arrest you, I think you can be bailed out fairly quickly depending on the judge."

"I don't want my wife and kids to know about this. Is that possible, at least for the time being?"

"Well it depends on the availability of the judge and the bail amount. We will try our best. But you know if this goes to trial, everybody will find out anyways."

"Yes, I understand. But we need to try for a settlement and keep it under wraps."

"Do you know if she has gone to an attorney? Let's hope that she has not. If she has, then settlement could be difficult and expensive."

"I don't know if she has or not, but at this point, nothing would surprise me."

"Well we better not waste time. Now you can call home and ask your wife for the phone number the policemen left for you to call them".

"Yes, she has been calling me and I have not taken her calls".

"Hello, Zainub?"

"Where are you? I have been calling and calling. There were two policemen who came to our house. I am so scared, where are you?"

"Look there is business problem. I will take care of it. You don't worry. Did they leave a number for me to call them back?" He took the number from his wife and gave it to Nancy. She called immediately.

"Oh, hi Sargeant Taylor, my name is Nancy Sweeney. I am calling in the matter of Mr. Salman Farook. I would like to make my client available for questioning, whenever it's convenient for you."

"He needs to be here, at the precinct within half hour. We are in process of issuing an arrest warrant for him," Sgt. Taylor replied. He was not a happy camper.

"Yes sir, we will be there in half an hour."

Salman was beginning to feel the gravity of the situation. When they got to the station, Sergeant Bill Taylor and Sergeant Robert Smith were waiting for them.

"Mr. Farook, you have the right to remain silent. Anything you say can and will be used against you in a court of law. You have a right to an attorney. If you cannot afford an attorney, one will be appointed for you. You are under arrest for the charges of rape and intentional misuse of authority of a subordinate."

After he had been Mirandized, Salman was handcuffed by one of the officers, and was taken away to a holding cell. Salman gave Nancy a look of helplessness. She gave him a look to stay calm. After Salman was taken to the holding cell, Nancy met with the officers and got more information about the victim's claims, her attorney's contact and whatever else she could. She was then allowed to meet with her client to strategize his bail and release.

"Mr. Farook, I want you to know that this is not going to be an easy case and I want you to be prepared for a tough fight. She has hired an attorney, and they have leveled some serious charges against you. I am going to get a bail hearing for you as quickly as I can. Since they have confiscated all your belongings, do you want me to call your wife? If I do, I must tell her the truth."

Salman had no choice, she had to know where he was, if he was not coming home. He told Nancy to go ahead and call her. *"But please tell her to keep it to herself and not let the children know."*

Sweeney was an experienced criminal attorney and was easily able to get a bail hearing for the next day. The judge set the bail for two hundred and fifty thousand dollars. Salman was out but seething with anger with what this Syrian family had put him through. The family for whom, in his mind, he had done so much. Sweeney picked up Salman to take him to her office to talk.

"I have some good news and some bad. The good news is that the attorney she has hired is not a criminal attorney. The bad news is that they don't want to settle. But don't worry, they all say that at first about settlement. Eventually they all settle when the settlement amount gets higher."

"So how did my wife take the news? What did she say?"

"To tell you the truth, I didn't understand most of what she said, but she wasn't crying or anything like I expected."

"I have a lot of explaining to do when I get home. I hope she hasn't told the children, that would be just too embarrassing to bear."

After arriving at Sweeney's office, they were joined by one of Sweeney's associate who was helping Sweeney on this case. *"So Mr. Farook, we need to get our ducks in a row and be prepared for every scenario that the plaintiff will throw at us. First of all, we have to wait until they officially file the charges. Once they do that, we will respond promptly. Of course our basic position is that this was between two consenting adults. I also know that you would like to settle but we should be prepared for the worst case scenario, which is going to a trial."*

Salman started shaking his head, *"No, no, no. No trial. We don't want a trial. We need to settle, whatever it takes."*

Nancy, although taken aback a little said, *"Ok, I will do my best. I can't guarantee that a settlement will be reached, but I have always been able to eventually settle."*

When Salman got home, he was relieved to hear that his wife had not told the children, that their father was in jail. *"How could you do this to me? What if someone finds out that Salman Farook is a rapist?"*

"Don't talk like that Zainub, it's just that I had too much to drink, and that bitch was encouraging me all along. Now she has changed her tune. I bet you somebody must have put her up to this, so that she could make a quick buck. Can you believe it? After all what we have done for them. I didn't expect this from Joseph and Selma. I haven't talked to Joseph, but Selma definitely had a different tone with me on the phone."

"Can you talk to Joseph? May be he could put some sense into those sisters," Zainub suggested.

"That's a good idea. Look, don't worry about what people will say, and all that. Our community gossipers will have a field day if this gets out. I have told Nancy to hurry up and settle. I won't be able to show my face if the kids find out."

"You should have thought about it before this foolishness," Zainub mumbled under her breath.

Salman called Joseph the next day. Joseph sounded profusely apologetic on the phone. Salman suggested meeting him at his office which Joseph agreed to.

"Mr. Salman, I'm really very sorry for what happened." Those were the first words that came out of Joseph's mouth when they met. *"I wish she wouldn't have involved the police. I feel so bad, this is terrible."*

"Joseph, you have known me for so many years. Haven't I been always been good to your family? So this is how your family pays me back? I have not been through so much shame in my entire life. You must know that in everything that happened, your sister-in-law was an equal participant. She and I went for lunches dozens of times, just the two of us alone. She used to tell me how she enjoyed my company and sent encouraging signals. She used to say that her late husband was about my age and that she prefers older men. She used to tell me how older men are more mature, more sophisticated and all that bullshit. So now I am wondering why was she saying all those things? Was she playing games with me or was it a setup?"

Joseph already suspected most of what Salman was saying. *"Mr. Salman I wouldn't have brought her here to America if she had not gone through so many tragic events. She has always been flirtatious, even her late husband knew it and didn't like it. My wife is very close to her, and whenever I say something, she comes to her defense. I don't know what to do."*

Salman was glad to see that at least Joseph had not turned against him like his wife. He was encouraged that at least there was some hope. *"So do you know Joseph, who is this lawyer she has hired, and where did she find him?"*

"His name is John Foster. He is the one who is handling our immigration issues. He got us all our green cards. We still don't have our citizenships, and he is handling that. He is very friendly with Sophia, and she has visited him a few times."

Joseph's last comments made Salman raise his eyebrows. *"What? That's unethical. An attorney can't take advantage of his client. How old is he? What else do you know about him?"*

"Well, he's about your age. He has a big office in downtown. His wife died a few years ago of cancer and he seems to be

very fond of Sophia. Look, Mr. Salman I don't want to get into any trouble with him. Just like you, he also has been very good to us, and I still owe him a lot of money."

"Joseph, you are a good man. You are the kind of person who doesn't forget to appreciate when someone helps you. I appreciate that and I respect that."

"Mr. Salman, John Foster is a good man, but you know when a woman is involved, people change. What happened is that Sophia called him, after that incident, and went to see him directly before coming home. He is the one who called the police. I think Sophia had told him about you and he must have thought it was a good chance to get you into trouble. This is just my guess."

"Joseph, I think you are right. Thank you for telling me all this. Don't worry, I am no longer upset with you, because whatever happened, you had nothing to do with it. You have painted a clear picture for me. Please stay in touch, and let me know if you find out anything new."

Jose was in the office working when Joseph came. They acknowledged each other, and Salman shut the door behind him. Jose still didn't know why Sophia had stopped coming to work, so when Joseph left, he couldn't wait to find out what was going on. He went to Salman's office. *"So boss, why has Sophia stopped coming to work?"*

"Jose, I am afraid you are going to have to be on your own for a while. There were some problems with Sophia and she is not coming back, but don't worry, I am going to get you some help soon." Salman didn't want to get into details with Jose.

Salman wanted to pass all the information to Nancy that he had received from Joseph. When he got hold of her, he started by saying, *"Guess what? The bitch has been sleeping with her lawyer."*

"What? What are you talking about"?

Salman told her everything that Joseph had told him.

"Well Mr. Farook, this is very useful information. Why is Joseph providing all this information to you? What's in it for

him? It seems like he is going against his own wife. Also, why is he giving all this information about the lawyer who's been good to him? Looks fishy to me."

"Nancy, there are still some good people left in this world. He is a good man. He feels obligated to help me because I have been good to him. He owes me thousands of dollars in back rent. I have helped him a lot in the past."

"Well that's good, but I am your lawyer; it's my job to be cynical and protect my client from suspicious characters. If your assumptions prove to be correct, he would definitely be an asset for our side."

***

When Joseph went home after work, Selma was anxiously waiting to talk to him, since she knew that he had gone to see Salman. He quickly let her know that he would only talk to her in private after dinner. Good to his word, when they were alone, he let her know what happened with Salman.

"Just like I suspected, your sister was totally involved in everything. Did she tell you that they used to go for lunches all the time? She used to encourage Salman by saying how she likes older men, how they are matured and sophisticated and all that. What is a man supposed to do? And above all, you and I both know how she feels about Muslims."

Selma didn't like what she was hearing. She lashed out, *"You have never liked her. You are always blaming my sister for everything. You have said so many things to me about her that weren't true. After all that she has gone through, I can't believe my own husband can be so cold hearted. How can you be so naive? Of course Salman is going to say all those things. Can't you see that? What's he going to say? I was waiting for an opportunity to rape an innocent woman"?*

Now Joseph was also upset, *"I don't like the tone of your voice. You are not going to talk to me in that manner. I will* not be disrespected by my wife in my own house. Besides, everything you just said was absurd. If I didn't sympathize with her, why would I work so hard to bring her here? Why would I give her a place in my house to live?"

"Well this is my house too," Selma yelled back.

Joseph had enough, "Okay, I think I have helped her enough. She's been here for more than two years, she needs to find her own place."

Selma didn't want to back down, "If she leaves, I will leave." She started crying.

Joseph wrapped his hands around her and tried to calm her down.

Their yelling had gotten loud enough for Sophia to hear in her room. The next morning when they were alone she asked Selma about the argument.

"Look Sophia, you are my sister and I love you very much, but it would be helpful if you always tell me the truth. Salman told Joseph things that you didn't tell me."

"What did he say?" Sophia had a concerned look on her face.

"Well that you were coming on to him with statements like older men are sophisticated and older men are this and that. It's not nice to encourage people like that; they can get all kinds of ideas." Selma's motherly instincts took over.

"Whatever I said, I definitely didn't want that to happen. But you are right, I will try to be more open with you in the future," Sophia promised.

Selma felt good about what she heard. "You know I am always open and honest with you, right? Joseph did say things last night that I don't think he meant. I think he said those things because he was angry."

Sophia had a worried look again, "What did he say?"

"He said that he had helped you enough, and now you should be on your own. I was so mad when I heard that, I told him, 'if she leaves I will go with her'."

55

"Oh no, don't say that. I would never let that happen. Are you out of your mind? You have such a great family, a loving husband and a great kid. Don't you even think about jeopardizing it. Joseph has done a lot for me, in spite of the fact that he doesn't like me very much. I appreciate what he has done. I will always be grateful. I was at the lowest ebb of my life, when you and he picked me up. I hope he didn't mean everything he said".

"Yeah, I don't think he meant it," Selma assured her.

***

A week later Salman received a call from Nancy Sweeney. "They have formally leveled rape charges against you, together with misuse of authority of an employer over his subordinate. I want you to know, Mr. Farook, that these are very serious charges. In all of their charges, the only surprise for me was the mention of condoms. You had never mentioned them to me".

"Why is that important? And, I am not even sure if she saw them." Salman wanted to know.

"Why would you say she didn't see them? Did she pass out?"

"No, she didn't pass out. But why is it important? Isn't it normal that when a man and a woman decide to have sex, and they don't want the woman to get pregnant, the man wears condoms? I thought that was a responsible thing to do."

"Under normal circumstances that would be a responsible thing to do, but yours was not a normal circumstance. You want to show the court that what happened was impulsive. You both had a few drinks, you both got tipsy and ended up having sex. On the other hand, having condoms there, shows intent. It shows that you were already planning it. It will just make it harder to convince the jury."

Salman dreaded words like juries and trials. "I thought I told I don't want it to go to trial."

Nancy responded quickly, *"And I told you that I will try, but there is no guarantee. Settlement is our goal, I understand that, but to reach a settlement amount I will have to negotiate. What if they want fifty million dollars, will you give it to them? Of course not. We don't know yet what they want."*

Salman was not finished yet on this subject. *"Look, you know this better than me. Jury trials are so unpredictable. Her lawyer will have no problem convincing the jurors how much of a victim she is, poor woman her husband and her child were killed by Muslims. Now another Muslim took advantage of her, right here in our own country. Remember she is a Christian and most jurors, if not all, will be Christians. I will be hammered from all sides."*

Nancy had her own arguments. *"The points you raise are all valid, but don't forget immigration nowadays is not so popular, and she is a new immigrant. Another fact is that she came from the Middle East, which is always a volatile area in people's mind. Just because she is woman doesn't mean she gets a pass. Recently a woman immigrant, who came from the Middle East, turned out to be a terrorist living in San Bernardino. Anyways, I will call the opposing lawyer, Foster, soon and get back to you."*

Salman was more worried and restless than he had ever been in his life. He couldn't sleep at night and knew Zainub was aware of his mental state. He kept apologizing to her for his shenanigans and she kept patiently telling him, that she would pray for him.

Salman was hoping against all hope that maybe Sophia would come to her senses and drop the charges. Although he strongly believed that the whole thing was consensual, he was realistic enough to know that, under the circumstances, it would be hard to prove. He called Joseph again to see if anything had changed, as far as her mindset was concerned.

8

"No, Mr. Salman, nothing has changed. I even had a big fight with my wife over this. I was so mad at Sophia, I wanted to kick her out of the house, but my wife said if I take that action she will leave with her. Now you tell me, what can I do?"

"Look Joseph, do me a favor, you need you to talk to your wife. Tell her that if she can talk Sophia into dropping the charges, Mr. Salman is willing to forgive the debt of six thousand dollars that we owe him, and on top of that he will also give Sophia five thousand dollars and she can also have her job back. Let's forgive and forget. What do you think Joseph, is that a good deal?"

"I feel bad, Mr. Salman, that you are willing to do all this, even after you have done so much for us already, but I will talk to her."

"Call me back and let me know what she says. You see, Joseph, this is a lot of money. You understand that, right?"

"I will call you back in a few minutes, they are both home. Let me call them right away."

Salman thought that this might be enough of an incentive for Joseph and Selma to get rid of their debt to him, and maybe they would put pressure on Sophia to drop the charges. He was going to keep his fingers crossed.

Joseph called home, "Selma, I have something to tell you. Salman just made a very generous offer to us, but it's only you, who make can this happen."

"What is it?" Selma was eager to find out.

"If you can talk Sophia into dropping the charges, we won't have to pay Salman all the money we owe him. We owe him six thousand dollars. On top of that, he is also willing to give Sophia five thousand dollars and her job back."

"I don't know Joseph, but let me ask her and I will call you back."

After talking to Sophia, Selma called Joseph back, *"She says she will talk to Mr. Foster first, before she gives an answer."*

Joseph was not happy with that answer but it was not in his control, *"You really have one hell of a selfish sister, you know that? After all we've done for her, the one time she can do something for us and she won't do it."*

Selma came to her defense again, *"Well she feels very strongly about it."*

"Strongly my foot, she is just selfish, pure and simple," he said before hanging up.

Joseph gave the bad news to Salman, who although disappointed, still saw some ray of hope that his proposal was not rejected outright.

Salman felt the walls closing in on him. Out of sheer desperation, he decided to call Foster himself. *"My name is Salman Farook. I'm the man you have falsely accused. I would like to talk to you."*

Foster was flabbergasted that an accused rapist would have the nerve to call him directly.

"Does your attorney know that you are calling me? Do you have any idea how inappropriate this is?"

Salman was desperate; he knew he shouldn't be doing this. *"Forget about my attorney, do you want to talk or not"?*

"No, I don't want to talk to you, you scumbag. If you have something to say, say it through your attorney. I'm not going to waste my time with you." Foster knew he was desperate.

"I know you have been sleeping with her, and I will make sure the American Bar Association knows that. You bring in innocent immigrant women and take advantage of them."

"Listen, you motherfucker Paki, you better get off the phone. You don't know who you are dealing with here. I would love to see you rot in jail for a long time. Hope you have a miserable day." Foster hung up.

Salman knew as soon as the phone call ended, that he made a serious mistake by calling Foster. He realized Sweeney would be pissed when she found out. He knew that he had made Foster so mad that he would tell Sophia not to drop charges. Somewhere in the back of his mind, he had initially thought that since all attorneys are crooks, he wanted to test Foster. The combination of his desperation and taking a chance to test Foster backfired on him.

Soon after Foster hung up with Salman, he heard from Sophia.

"Hi Sophia, how are you? Nice to hear from you. What's happening?"

"Mr. Foster, I wanted to ask you something."

"Remember, I told you to call me John."

"Oh yeah, I forgot. John. I wanted to ask you, is it Okay, if drop we the charges? I mean Salman has been calling a lot. He told Joseph that he would forgive their back rent and give me five thousand and my job back blah blah blah."

"That son of a bitch has been calling everybody. He just called me too. Look, I personally think it would be a mistake to drop the charges. If you do that, he would get off cheap and it will be a mockery of justice. After all the injustices you have endured in your life, do you really want to squash the one opportunity afforded to you? Look, being your lawyer, I have a binding duty to do what you want, but, I have to give you the most reasonable, logical, and legal advice."

"John, I personally don't want to drop the charges, but I want to help my sister too. Salman said if I drop the charges, she would not have to pay the back rent. If I don't drop the charges, my sister will think I don't want to help her." Sophia sounded confused.

"Sophia, hear me out. Salman is a very deceitful and sinister individual. I deal with people like him every day. Don't be fooled by the games he is playing. He is trying to pit you against your sister. Tell your sister that if we decide to settle, he

would be willing to fork out not a few thousand, but hundreds of thousands. He is a very rich individual and there is a lot at stake here for him. He could go to jail for a very long time. People like him would do anything to avoid going to jail."

Sophia felt empowered. *"Okay John, I understand now. I don't want to drop the charges."*

"Good then, I am glad. So when are going to come and visit me?" Foster thought he finally got her in a good mood.

"When do you want me to come? I don't go to work anymore."

Foster glanced at his calendar quickly, *"How about next Thursday? That seems like a slower day."*

"Okay, I will come around lunch time."

Next thing Foster wanted to do was to put the brakes on Salman's activities. He got hold of Nancy Sweeney.

"Are you aware of your client's shenanigans? I'm letting you know, you better put him on a leash, he is running wild—totally out of control."

"I don't know what you are talking about. What did he do?" Nancy sensed something was wrong.

"Well, he called me directly instead of going through his attorney, started to threaten me and accuse me of all kinds of nonsense. He is also calling my client and trying to manipulate her family by offering them deals and basically creating havoc in their lives. You better make him aware that this is not Pakistan, this is United States, things work differently over here." Foster was furious.

"Calm down a little John. I agree he shouldn't have called you. I will make sure that it doesn't happen again. As far as calling your client is concerned, as you know, she lives at his tenant's residence. He owns that place, for God's sake. He may have called there to collect rent, maybe something is broken, it could be anything. But I will find out. I agree however, that he shouldn't try to talk to your client. Also, I would appreciate it if you refrain from disparaging my client's nationality."

"And he shouldn't be offering deals in a legal matter without my client's attorney being present." Foster had to put the last word in. Both attorneys realized they had a tough case ahead of them.

Sweeney was furious at Salman after finding out what he was doing. She called him right after hanging up with Foster. *"Mr. Farook, do you want my firm to continue representing you?"*

"Yes of course. What kind of question is that?" Salman knew Nancy was upset.

"Well then, you are going to have to cease all your solo activities on legal matters immediately, or we will withdraw ourselves from representing you, and you can find other representation." Nancy was blunt.

"Are you threatening me? I don't like threats." Salman tried to play tough.

"No, I am not threatening you. I am telling you that we will not represent you if you will not follow the attorney-client rules, take it or leave it. Now please tell me, which will it be?"

"Okay, okay, I get it." Salman didn't want to lose the only people trying to help him.

***

After the conversation Sophia had with Foster she was sure that she didn't want Salman to get off easy. Now she had to face Selma, who had her hopes high that they could get rid of the big debt they owed Salman. That could only happen if Sophia would drop the charges.

"Selma, I am so sorry. Foster doesn't want me to drop the charges."

"But I thought that it was supposed to be your decision, and he was supposed to do what you want," Selma said, disappointment written all over her face.

"Yes, he and I talked about it in detail, and it's best if I don't. I am so sorry to disappoint you."

"But why? I don't understand. Don't you want this thing to be over with? Don't you want to leave it behind? Why would you want to drag this on? Salman regrets it. He made a mistake, wants to pay for his mistake and now wants to move on. You don't see it that way?"

"No, I don't see it that way. I don't want him to get off so easily. Look Selma, I have leftover money that I brought from Syria, I can give you six thousand dollars to pay him off."

"Oh no, we can't take your money. You must save that money for emergency purposes. This is a new country for us, you never know what might happen. But what I don't understand is why you want to punish him, so bad?" Selma couldn't figure it out.

"It's very simple Selma, but I don't think I will be able to make you understand. What his people, have done to me and my family, I will never forgive. This is my chance to give him a little taste of what pain is."

Selma didn't agree. *"I don't know why you keep saying his people. He is not even from the Middle East. Just because was he was born in that religion? And, he doesn't even practice it. This is crazy."*

Sophia wouldn't listen, *"As far as I am concerned they are all the same. Savages. You won't understand it because you haven't gone through what I went through. I still have nightmares that I don't share with you or anyone else."*

***

Although Danny had some suspicion as to what was going on, he wasn't exactly sure. He was however, concerned about the frequent yelling between his parents. When he got a chance he asked his dad, *"Why are you two fighting all the time?"*

Joseph was taken aback a little and got defensive, *"We don't fight. When did you see us fighting?"*

"Dad, come on, just because your bedroom door is closed doesn't mean no one can hear you when you are shouting. The doors are not sound proof, for God's sake."

"Okay, okay, I will tell you, you're not a kid anymore. Look, your Aunt Sophia is creating a lot of problems for us, and your mother is always defending her."

"But she is mom's sister, and she is all alone. Dad, how can you not have sympathy for her after what she has been through?"

"My boy, I do have sympathy for her. Who do you think brought her here? Whose house is she living in rent-free for more than two years? I just want you to know what really took place that your mom doesn't want to hear."

"Okay, tell me."

"Well you know uncle Salman gave her a job in his office? He figured she was new in the country, she would learn about America, make some money, good for everybody right? Salman also has an office manager. The all three of them would go out for lunch sometimes. Sometimes when the office manager was out collecting rent or something, only uncle Salman and your aunt would go. You know your aunt is a beautiful woman. One day they had a little too much to drink, things got out of hand and they did something they wouldn't have done if they were sober."

"Wow, isn't uncle Salman much older? So is she embarrassed, mad? Because he's older or what? I mean they were both involved, right?"

"See, now that's an honest thing to say, which you did. But that's not how both the sisters see. They are saying, no, because he is a man, he tricked her into drinking, he had planned all this to get into her pants. The entire fault is his, and she is just an innocent victim. Now you tell me, how is that fair? These are not just verbal accusations, now she has hired a

lawyer and wants to put Uncle Salman in jail. I'm sure you know he had always been good to us. I owe him a lot of back rent. He has also helped me with this business. How I can turn my back on him just like that? Your mother used to invite Salman and Zainub to the house. She used to say nice things about them and now all of a sudden he is a devil."

Danny understood his dad, but he didn't want to say anything bad about his mom. *"Well dad, Mom just loves her sister too much. As they say, sometimes love is blind."*

Joseph was satisfied that at least his son understood his dilemma.

That night, when Selma and Joseph were alone in their bedroom, Selma broke the news that Sophia was not going to drop the charges. Of course it meant that they still owed the back rent.

"What is wrong with your sister? Why is she hell bent on destroying his reputation? Doesn't she know that this is something she could have done for us, and it would have helped us out tremendously? The one time she could do something for us and she won't do it. Oh my God, she is crazier than I thought."

Selma didn't have the energy to fight back, she was tired and wanted to go to sleep. But Joseph was not done. *"Look if she doesn't have the decency to avail an opportunity to help us out, I am under no obligation to help her anymore. Please tell her to start looking for a place of her own."*

Selma didn't threaten to move out with her sister this time. However, she wanted to tell Joseph about the offer her sister had made, *"Sophia is willing to give us the six thousand we owe Salman, so that we can get him off our backs."*

"I don't want her money, she can keep it. She can use that for her moving expenses," Joseph said sarcastically.

***

Jose was still in the dark. Salman never felt the need to tell him why Sophia suddenly stopped coming to work. One day he just couldn't resist the curiosity, so he called Sophia himself. She did take his call this time, *"Hi Sophia, how are you? Are you okay?"*

For a few seconds Sophia wasn't sure if it was Salman who was having Jose call her, but she decided to answer anyways. *"I am fine, how are you?"*

"Can you talk on the phone, or you would feel more comfortable if I come and see you? I know where you live."

"Did Salman ask you to call me?"

"No, I'm calling on my own."

"Ok come over, I will wait for you."

When Jose arrived he gave her a big hug. They were both happy to see each other. Jose had been in the dark, but he was about to find out. *"I missed you so much. Salman never told me why you stopped coming. I figured there must be a reason why he doesn't want to tell me. He keeps telling me he will get me help, but I don't know when. I am overwhelmed. I can use some help."*

"Jose, I am sorry you have to do all the work. You know, you had warned me about him, I should have listened to you."

"Oh no! What happened? What did he do?"

"You know we never had any drinks whenever he took us out for lunch right?"

"Right."

"Well, one day when you were out, he took me to that Thai restaurant that I like, and ordered a bottle of wine. He kept pouring in my glass and when we went back to the office, he took advantage of me. I believe he had planned all that ahead of time."

Jose was shocked. *"Oh my God. So what are you going to do? Are you asking for money?"*

"Well I have filed a case against him. I don't care about money. I want to teach him a lesson."

Jose suddenly realized that he should be at the job. *"Ok Sophia, I have to go, I don't want him to know that I am talking to you. Please take care of yourself. It was nice seeing you."*

***

Joseph continued to feel frustrated because of his inability to help Salman. He had heard horrible stories about how cold hearted landlords could be, but Salman was nothing like that. He wanted to let him know that Sophia had not accepted his offer.

"Mr. Salman, I am sorry to tell you that Sophia won't budge. My wife tried to put some sense into her; she refuses to listen even to her own sister. I am so angry with her. I have asked her to find her own place."

Salman remembered his scolding from Sweeney; that he was not supposed to be talking to anyone about this subject. *"Okay Joseph, thanks for letting me know. But tell me one thing. Do you have any idea why is she doing this to me? Haven't I been good to all of you? Why then? Why is she so determined to destroy me?"*

"I am not sure, but I have an idea." Joseph said softly. *"I think it's because her husband and her daughter were both killed by Muslim fanatics, and now she hates all Muslims. Since you are a Muslim, maybe she is getting some kind of satisfaction out of hurting you."*

"But if that's the case, then why work for me? Why even be near me? Why go out for lunches with me? I don't get it. This is crazy."

It was extremely hard for Selma to tell her sister what Joseph had said. *"Are you sure sweetie you won't change your mind? You know, Joseph was very upset when he heard you had decided not to drop the charges."*

"I am sorry Selma, I have made up my mind. Did you tell him I am willing to pay the debt he owes Salman?"

"Yes, I did. We both knew he wasn't going to take the money from a woman, he is too proud. But he asked me again to tell you to start looking for a place."

"Well, if that's what he wants then I will just have to find a place of my own. I am sorry, Selma that it has come to this. We are being separated, but I feel that I am doing the right thing. I am having lunch with Mr. Foster tomorrow, maybe he can help me find an affordable place."

***

The court date for Salman to appear in front of the judge was only a week away. He was getting more and more nervous. He had tried everything he could think of to turn the situation in his favor. He called Nancy to find out if there was anything new.

"No, Mr. Farook, there are no new development in your case. I have left a message for John Foster to call me back to discuss settlement, but again I want to remind you that you should prepare yourself for the worst case scenario. Sometimes the plaintiffs are just not willing to listen to any logic and are hell bent on going to trial."

"But what would they gain by going to trial? Aren't they taking a risk that they might lose in the trial, and hence lose the settlement amount being offered?" Salman wanted to know.

"Yes, you are right, they're taking that risk, but the reasons vary, as to why they are taking that risk. Some plaintiffs do it because the risk-reward ratio is very much in their favor. Some do it because the animosity/hatred towards the defendant is too strong and they just want to see him convicted."

Salman was dreading to ask this question, but went ahead anyway, *"What do you think our chances are in a trial? Do you have any idea as to how much they will ask to settle?"*

"The way it works is that I will try my best to negotiate and figure out the lowest amount they are willing to settle for, then I get your approval. This is assuming they are willing to settle in the first place. Nothing happens without their willing to settle or your approval. As far as my own impression about the opposing

lawyer, he is like any other lawyer. He seems competent. He was pretty pissed off at you though, the other day."

"Well I learned my lesson, I shouldn't have done that," Salman admitted.

"Mr. Farook, while we are waiting for Foster to call me, please start your own preparations. Start gathering any physical evidence, photos, letters, emails, texts, computer records etc. We want to show to the court that you had a friendly relationship with her. One more thing, you mentioned you have another guy working in the office right?"

"Yes, he is the office manager Jose. He's been with me for several years. Very nice guy."

"Well we may need Jose. Make sure you keep him happy," Nancy instructed.

Salman's nervousness didn't diminish at all after talking to his lawyer. In all the forty some years he had been in United States, he had never been in such a predicament. He felt so helpless. He had always been in awe of the United States justice system, but now he was going to see it up close and personal. He didn't have a choice but to start preparing at least mentally, what might happen. He started making a list of the things Nancy had mentioned, including being nice to Jose.

Salman had not been going to the office lately, leaving everything for Jose to take care of. After what Nancy said about Jose, he went to the office the next day.

"How's everything going Jose? Sorry I have been preoccupied the last few days."

Jose knew what the preoccupation was but pretended as if he didn't know anything. *"That's okay boss, I know you are a busy person, lots of meetings and businesses to take care of. I have things under control."*

"Jose, I know I can always depend on you. You have always been a trustworthy employee." Salman started to do his groundwork.

Jose sensed that something was up. He was not used to hearing stuff like that from Salman.

"Look Jose, since you are carrying two people's load, I have decided to increase your salary by 20%. I want to make sure that you're compensated according to what you deserve."

Jose was delirious. He immediately gave up trying to analyze the reasons behind all this. He was just happy. *"Thank you, Mr. Salman. You're very kind."*

Salman decided that this was the right time to bring up the other subject. *"Jose, I never told you what happened to your co-worker. Today I will tell you. You know, I always try to help people, especially the newcomers to this country. I helped you; I helped Joseph and his family. I have helped many more people, who you don't even know. The reason why it is important to me is that when I was a newcomer myself, no one helped me, and I had to struggle a lot. So I decided to help Sophia also. I thought it would be good for her, she would learn the American system. You know, if it wasn't for me, nobody would have hired her. She didn't know anything. You agree?"*

Jose shook his head affirmatively.

Salman continued. *"Well, she worked here for over two years, learned everything and the three of us became close. We went out for lunch frequently, it was always my treat and we enjoyed ourselves. Right?"*

Again Jose shook his head affirmatively.

"Jose, you must have noticed that sometimes we teased each other, told jokes to each other, and the jokes were not always clean. She used to call me a dirty old man sometimes, and then I in turn, called her names. I didn't mind all that, although I was the boss and she was my employee, because all three of us were like close friends."

Jose just listened and didn't shake his head this time. He knew exactly what Salman was up to.

***

Foster finally returned Sweeney's call.

"*What can I do for you Miss Sweeney*"?

"*Well, our preliminary hearing is coming up, and I am sure judge Malcolm is going to ask us if the opposing attorneys have discussed the case amongst each other.*"

"*I agree that the judge will expect that. What would you like to discuss? We think our case is cut and dry. Salman is an employer; he should have used better judgment. He misused his authority, got his subordinate drunk and raped her.*"

"*Wait, wait, Mr. Foster, not so fast. Nobody was raped. Nobody forced Sophia to do anything. She is a beautiful woman and she's flirtatious. She had been coming on to my client for a long time. They'd been going to these lunches for a while. This one time, things got out hand, but everything was consensual.*"

"*Miss Sweeney, I am sure you know the laws and guidelines that govern how an employer must behave during working hours. I have no doubt those laws and guidelines apply in this case,*" Foster insisted.

Sweeney knew that it would be a challenging trial, and she liked challenges, but her hands were tied. Her client did not want to go to trial. "*Mr. Foster, we can go on about this forever, but we have to face Judge Malcolm soon. As you probably know, this judge insists on opposing attorneys communicating with each other. That's what I am trying to do. He is also going to ask us if we tried to get to some common ground. Can we try to agree on some things?*"

"*I think, in a roundabout way, you are trying to ask me if we're willing to settle. Am I right?*" Foster was not a novice at this.

"*Yes. But if you are not interested, we can move on to whatever we need to do next.*" Sweeney didn't like to be cornered.

Foster was smiling. He knew Salman was probably cringing at the idea of coming to a settlement. "*The last time I spoke with my client about her case, she was not interested in a settlement,*" *but I can ask again. Do you have a figure in mind that I can tell her?"* Foster was curious to know how badly they wanted this.

Sweeney was not about to fulfill his curiosity so easily. *"Well talk to her and let us know if she changes her mind about settling, because if not, we think we have a strong case."*

They hung up, both knowing they had an uphill battle.

***

Salman was slowly coming to terms that his desire to push this under the rug was not likely. *Having a rape charge around his neck sounded so horrible and disgusting. What would the people in his community think? His wife would be so ashamed to answer questions from other community women. How would he face his children? Would they even understand?*

Salman's wife, who had good a relationship with Selma, had not talked to her for a long time. She decided to give her a call to see if something could be done.

"Hello Selma, this is Zainub, how are you?"

Selma figured this might be another of Salman's tricks, but she liked Zainub. *"Oh I am fine. Nice to hear from you. How have you been? How are the kids?*

After the initial chitchat, Zainub came straight to the point, *"Selma, can't you get your sister to stop what she is doing? Can't you see how we tried to help her? And now she is doing this to us."*

Selma didn't like Zainab's tone. *"Look Zainub, I like you and I respect you, but you're talking about my sister here. She is doing this because she believes your husband violated her dignity. How would you feel if I called you and talked to you about your sister this way? Please have some respect. I know we owe you some money, and you will be paid but that doesn't mean we will tolerate your insults."*

They hung up. Zainub had never seen this side of Selma before. *You learn something new every day, Wow, how people change, Zainub was saying to herself.*

***

Sweeney needed to inform Salman that Foster was playing hard ball and there was no progress on the settlement talks. *"Mr. Farook, I wanted to let you know that the opposing side is not prepared to talk about settlement."*

"Why, what happened? How much are they asking?" a dejected Salman asked.

"We haven't even started the numbers game yet. They weren't even ready to agree that there could be a settlement. Foster said he has to approach his client again. I don't want to appear too anxious, that would make us look weak." Sweeney gave him her justification.

"Miss Sweeney, I hate to say this, but we don't have much time to play games. You should have thrown a number out there to get the ball rolling and test the waters."

"With all due respect Mr. Farook, don't try to tell me how to do my job. I have been doing this for a long time. If they don't even utter the word settlement in the whole conversation, and avoid the subject deliberately, it doesn't do anybody any good. They will chew you up and spit you out and you won't even know what happened."

Salman was wondering if he made a mistake by hiring this woman as his attorney. She either didn't understand the gravity of the situation, or she was deliberately complicating the case to increase her fees and billable hours. But he felt trapped, he knew it was too late to bring somebody new in. *"I still would like you to keep trying. I just don't want to go to trial,"* Salman desperately pleaded.

9

Sophia went to see Foster on the Thursday they had talked about on the phone. Foster had told his secretary he would not be back after lunch. Sophia and Foster were happy to see each other.

"Great to see you, Sophia. How are you?"

"I am nervous. Too much going on. Things are moving too fast." Sophia knew Foster could always put her at ease with his words.

"Don't worry, you know I am here. You can always count on me. So what's bothering you today? I can sense something is wrong."

"You know John, when Joseph found out I was not dropping the charges, he was so mad, he is kicking me out from his house."

"Really? Wow. What did your sister say?"

"She is not happy, but I don't want her to breakup her marriage because of me."

"Does Joseph really want you out or he was just angry at the time? Usually he seems so calm."

"He is serious. He actually doesn't like me."

"Nah, how can anybody not like you? Isn't he the reason why you are here today? He used to come and sit in my office lobby, day after day, on your behalf."

"No, you are the reason why I'm here today. I'm sure my sister was pushing him like crazy."

"He never told me how pretty you were." Foster started teasing her.

She smiled shyly, "Should we go for lunch? I am hungry."

"Yes, give me five more minutes to finish something up. I am not coming back to the office after lunch."

"*Oh really?* Sophia was pleasantly surprised. *So what are we going to do after lunch?*"

"*I don't know. We can talk about it at lunch.*"

The subject of Sophia's moving came up again during lunch.

"*Look Sophia, you and I have known each other for a while and we both like each other, right?*"

"*Right,*" Sophia said softly, not knowing where he was going.

"*Well, I have a big house, not far from the beach, and I would love for you to move in with me. What do you think?*"

Foster didn't know that a woman living with an unmarried man in her culture was not acceptable. She was shocked that he had offered this arrangement. Then she realized that this was America, and she was determined not to worry about the culture that had given her nothing but misery and suffering. She listened to Foster's offer but was very unsure. "*I don't know what to say.*"

"*Let's wait for a while. Let's wait until the trial is over. Right now it's not going to look good.*"

Sophia shook her head affirmatively. "*I think you are right.*" Although she was tremendously happy at the prospect of living near the beach, and with someone she cared about, but she was also nervous about the unknowns.

After lunch they decided to go to John's house. She was impressed with how huge it was. The living room alone was bigger than the whole apartment where she was living. John proudly showed her around. At one point they were even holding hands, as if a young couple was being shown a house by a real estate agent. "*So what do you think?*" John asked.

"*It's a lovely house. This is the biggest house I have seen in America.*" Sophia was exuberant.

"*I was saving the best part for the last. Come with me. He held her hand and led her upstairs to a huge bedroom, where the curtains were drawn. OK now open the curtain.*"

When Sophia opened the curtain, she couldn't believe her eyes. There was a beautiful ocean view that was beyond describable. John opened the sliding glass door that led to the balcony. Sophia couldn't help herself; she was so overwhelmed that she ran into John's open arms. John kissed her softly for the first time.

"You want to know something Sophia? My wife passed away almost two years ago and this is the first time I have kissed another woman."

Sophia couldn't say anything, but she moved towards John, and it was her turn to kiss him.

"Would you like to go for a walk near the water?"

"Let's do that next time. I will bring some appropriate clothes."

"Hmm, a bikini maybe?" John teased.

"That I will need to buy. Maybe we will go shopping together." Sophia had always been good with flirting.

"That's a deal." John never dreamt he would feel this way again, much less at his age.

"I should be heading back. My sister must be wondering where I am. I told her I would be back after lunch."

"You can tell her we went looking for a place for you to live since Joseph wants you to leave."

"Hey, that's a good idea John. You are so smart."

"In my business you need to think fast," John tried to be funny.

They headed back down to the living room. Here they sat at a table and discussed some of the pertinent points in Sophia's case before she left. *"Sophia, I want to talk to you about your case, so let's get serious for a little while. This is important."*

Sophia was amazed at how quickly John could change his mood from romantic to business.

John started saying, *"Being your lawyer, I must..."*

She stopped him, putting a finger on his lips, *"You are not my lawyer anymore, you are something else."*

John smiled widely, *"Yes, but I still have to get your concurrence on everything, my dear."*

76

"Everything? I hope not." Now it was Sophia's turn to tease.

"Will you get serious for a few minutes please, sweetheart!"

"Oh, I like that, okay, okay. I will try to be serious now. "Sophia was enjoying it too much.

"So, this guy Salman's lawyer wants to know if we are willing to settle the case by dropping the charges. What do you think?"

"No. No way. I don't want to drop the charges. I want him to get the taste of some pain. He will never go through the pain I went through, but maybe a little bit."

"I know you're very angry, but don't forget in America it's not easy to incarcerate someone. There will be a long and slow battle, and, we might lose. He has a very good lawyer."

"I have full confidence in you. I know that for my sake, you will not let him go free. He must suffer like I did."

"Another thing I must tell you is that in these kinds of cases a lot of dirty laundry is going to come out. They will bring out a lot of sexually explicit and embarrassing things. Will you be able to handle them?"

"Yes, I am ready for anything, as long as I have you with me."

"Wow, you seem so determined. Is it because he a Muslim? Or is there something else? He is not even a Syrian."

"They all call themselves brothers. They are all the same."

"Sophia, I don't blame you. What you have gone through is unimaginable." Foster got his answer.

When Sophia got home, Selma was anxiously waiting for her little sister. She wanted to know how her date went. Sophia gave Selma a big hug as soon as she saw her. *"Oh Selma, I can't even describe to you how happy I am."* Joseph and Danny were not home from work yet, so they could talk freely.

Selma didn't expect that the date would go that well. *"Oh my goodness, are you okay?"*

"No, I am not okay. I am in love."

Sophia went on and on. She didn't stop until the guys came home.

The next day Sophia called Jose. The first thing she asked was if he was alone. He said he was. She told him her dilemma about finding a small place temporarily. He told her he would be more than happy to help. *"How are things at the office?"* she asked.

"Oh busy as usual. Salman hardly ever comes to the office." He told her how unhappy he appeared to be whenever he did see Salman. He also told her how he was trying to be nice to him.

Jose helped Sophia move into a small apartment not far from her current place. She didn't want to go too far from Selma, and wanted to stay in the familiar neighborhood. Selma started to cry when she was moving out. Sophia was the stronger one, she kept reminding her that she was close by, and they could drop in at each other's place as often as they wanted.

10

At the preliminary hearing both lawyers presented their cases in front of Judge Malcolm. The judge was informed that the opposing lawyers did communicate with each other before coming to him. The judge was also informed that the petitioner wished jury trial, and did not want to settle. After hearing both sides, the judge didn't have a choice but to grant at a trial. He set the jury selection date for two months from the preliminary hearings. He also allowed that the plaintiff could change her mind until the trial began.

As much as he had wanted otherwise, Salman had grudgingly accepted the fact that he would have to face the jury. His fate was going to be in the hands of twelve strangers. He would now see the American justice system up close and personal. He had thought about doubling his legal team but the offer was declined by Sweeney. He wasn't going to take any chances by disagreeing or aggravating Sweeney at this juncture.

Now Salman had to face another tough task. He had no choice but to tell his kids. He had been successful in hiding it from them so far, with his wife's cooperation. Salman had two grown children, Rashid and Razia, a son and a daughter. They were both married professionals, who had their own families with kids. He had always been a good father to them. He had worked very hard in cultivating a good image of himself in their eyes. They both thought highly of him. He was a man who had come to the U.S. from a backward country, a successful, self-made, businessman who had a good standing in the community.

Salman was terrified that all this would change if he didn't come up with a good story. He made the dreaded phone calls. Without being overly dramatic he asked them to come to his house for something urgent. He instructed them to come alone without their spouses or kids.

Salman's son and daughter had never heard their father speak that way before. They told him that they would take the following day off, to meet with him. All kinds of nervous thoughts were going through their minds. Did he find out he had cancer? Was he terminally sick? Was something wrong with Mom? Their questions would be answered the following day.

They sat together as a family, the four them, Salman, Zainub, Rashid and Razia. Salman started speaking. *"Look children, I am facing a big challenge. Probably the biggest of my life, and I need your support and understanding."* Both children looked at each other puzzled, still without a clue as to what's coming next.

"Pops, you are not sick, are you?" The son couldn't wait any longer.

Salman with a half-smile, shook his head sideways, *"No, no, I'm not sick."*

They shared a sigh of relief. *"Thank God,"* his daughter said out loud.

Salman continued. *"I have made many mistakes in my life, but none bigger than this one."* You both know Joseph and Selma right? The Syrian family who are renting one of my condos?"* They both shook their heads affirmatively. "Well, they also brought in another woman, Selma's sister, to live with them. I felt sorry for that woman and gave her a job at the office to help out Jose. Jose was overwhelmed with having so much to do by himself. He was doing all the paperwork as well as outside work, collecting rent and so forth. Well, you know me, I like to take care of my employees, so sometimes I used to take them out for lunch, to make them feel appreciated. Well one day, Jose was out, and that woman and I went for lunch. That was my mistake. I should've resisted drinking alone with her.*

"When we came back to the office, we were both tipsy. She kept coming on to me and, regretfully, the alcohol took over. I think it was a set up. I have been apologizing to your mother ever since, and now I want to apologize to you two, for letting you down. You know this is why our religion doesn't allow drinking. You lose your senses. You lose control of differentiating between right and wrong.

"This woman has now hired a high priced lawyer and is making ridiculous accusations that I raped her and what not. Can you believe that? No good deed goes unpunished, right? On top of that, she's extremely stubborn. She's won't listen to reason. She won't listen to her sister, her brother-in-law, anyone. She's hell bent on destroying me. So now, because of this stupid woman, I have to face a trial, and be ridiculed in front of the world. That is why I asked you two to come here, so that I can get it off my chest. I could care less about what the outside world thinks, but I do care what my kids think of me."

Salman's kids were flabbergasted with their dad's dilemma. They both believed everything he said, because they had such high regard for him.

"Pops, I am really sorry for what happened. I guess you are just too nice, and in today's world there are all kinds of people ready to take advantage of situations like this." He got up and gave his dad a big hug.

His daughter did the same stating, *"If I ever see her, I will break her neck."* She was furious at that woman who had placed her dad in this position.

Salman was happy that he was able to convince his children that he was a victim of a setup.

11

Sweeney had told Salman that she was planning to put three witnesses on the stand on his behalf. All three would need to be prepped by her, if they agreed to be the witnesses. She instructed him to contact the restaurant owner where he and Sophia had lunch before the incident, then talk to Jose and Joseph. The owner, Mr. Chanchai, knew Salman as a good customer for many years and he agreed to be a witness. Jose didn't show his reluctance outwardly, but was very skeptical.

Joseph's situation was tricky. He would have to potentially go against his wife and was also concerned about his relationship with Mr. Foster. But his anger and distaste towards Sophia had gone far beyond his reluctance, and he agreed to be a witness. Salman let Sweeney know that the three witnesses were ready for prepping.

Selma had a hard time adjusting to Sophia being away. She and Joseph started fighting more often. Instead of going to the store where she used to go to help out, now she was always at Sophia's place. That annoyed Joseph to no end.

Sophia was spending most of her time with Foster, including the weekends when he wasn't working. That was one big benefit that came from her moving from Joseph's house. No one was waiting for her anymore or wondering where she was when she went out. When alone, she often reflected on how many drastic twists and turns her life had taken. It would have been unimaginable to think just a few years ago, what she had gone through and how it would all end up in America.

She was also spending time familiarizing herself with the American laws, and helping Foster develop her case.

Salman had also started to collect all the records he could muster. There had been some electronic communications between him and Sophia, like texts and e-mails that needed sorting. He also instructed Jose to do the same with his own interactions with Sophia. He still didn't know that Jose had kept in touch with Sophia.

Salman found out from Joseph that Sophia had moved out of his home. He wouldn't dare antagonize Sweeney again by trying to contact Sophia or make any stupid moves. He thought that would be suicidal. He would however, take any voluntary information given by Joseph, and pass it on to Sweeney. In the meantime, Jose had called Sophia to let her know that he didn't have a choice but to be a witness for Salman and had profusely apologized. Sophia told him that she understood.

Foster and Sophia were also giving a lot of time and priority to the upcoming trial, collecting notes and evidence. The hospital report was not quite what Foster had hoped for, but he was not an expert on reading those kinds of medical reports. Looking at it from a non-expert point of view, it did not show any forcible sexual encounter or any traumatic tear of the area. A favorable report could have shown the jury the non-consensual nature of the encounter. But Foster had not given up on the report. He decided to hire an independent expert who would look at the report with his bias leaning towards the victim.

Foster and Sophia were equally determined to see Salman in jail. He wanted to leave no stone unturned to give her the satisfaction that she desired so much. He believed that what Sophia went through was a tragedy of the highest proportion, and now deserved happiness.

Sweeney was fairly confident that, with the right jurors, she could win. She knew that Salman was a loose cannon but also knew how to handle somebody like him. She had not quite decided yet if she would put him on the witness stand. She couldn't believe how disorganized he was, and was amazed at how he got to be so successful in business. Still, she met with him regularly and kept putting together whatever information he could come up with. She knew that her billable hours were not going to be a problem, since he had never shown any concern about the money being spent.

The jury selection for the case was not far away. She had already prepped the possible witnesses she was going to call. The one thing she had not yet discussed with him was the possible media attention this case had the potential of attracting. Normally it would be just another case, where an employee had accused her boss of abusing his authority. But this was different. Here, the religion component would come into play. A Muslim man accused of raping a Christian woman, right here in United States. A Christian-Syrian refugee accuses an American citizen of rape in United States. The press could have a field day with that kind of story. Although it could have brought in some good publicity for Sweeney and her firm, she knew her client would hate it.

12

Both attorneys were contentious to the nth degree, as expected, during the jury selection, but then finally the jury was seated.

Salman and Sophia saw each other for the first time since the incident, on the first day of trial. Both tried to avoid eye contact. Selma and Joseph were sitting behind Foster and Sophia. Sophia had never seen an American court room before. Although Foster had fully prepared her, she was still very nervous, but determined. Foster had requested the judge and Sweeney to allow him to put Sophia on the witness stand last. Both the judge and Sweeney had no objection to his request.

Salman sat next to Nancy Sweeney. Behind him were his wife Zainub and Jose. The twelve jurors and three alternates were seated on the side of the courtroom. The attorneys had selected seven women and five men for the jury quorum.

"Mr. Foster, let's hear your opening statement," the judge stated.

"Ladies and Gentlemen, we believe, that we can provide ample evidence in this case to the jury that Mr. Salman Farook is a manipulative, conniving and deceitful individual. In the guise of being helpful, he takes full advantage of the situation when it presents itself. We will prove to the jury that Mr. Farook, being an employer, used his direct authority over my client, directing her to go to lunch with him. We will prove that his sole purpose of hiring my client was to seduce her and take advantage of her at an opportune time. We will prove that he kept close tabs on the only third person in the office, Mr. Jose Lopez. He did that mainly, so he could take advantage of my client. Mr. Farook's conduct has been so outrageous and so out of control that he

even called me personally and tried to threaten me." Foster sat down after completing his opening statement.

"Miss Sweeney, the floor is yours for your opening statement," the judge directed.

"Honorable Judge and respected members of the jury, contrary to what you just heard, Mr. Salman is a decent and honorable man. He is an outstanding citizen with an impeccable reputation and enviable standing in the community. He has no prior history with law enforcement. We will show to the jury that the plaintiff is a clever, manipulative, and calculating woman. We will show that she has a history of flaunting her good looks to use men. We will prove that she has a history of being flirtatious and deceptive. We will show that Sophia Delgado, instead of being grateful to a man who has been good to her and to her family, is now trying to destroy him." Sweeney sat down after her opening statement.

Sophia couldn't believe the harshness of the things she heard Sweeney say about her. She expected some unpleasantness, but not to this extent. *She started to wonder, if this was just the beginning, then what's more to come? She now understood why Foster had warned her.*

The judge asked Mr. Foster to call his first witness. *"I call Selma Mendes to take the stand,"* Foster said.

This was the Selma's first experience in court. She was tense but determined to do anything for her sister.

"Please state your name and your relationship with the plaintiff for the record."

"My name is Selma Mendes and I am Sophia's sister."

"Mrs. Mendes, do you know Mr. Salman Farook?"

"Yes, I know him, he is our landlord."

"Mrs. Mendes, do you have a restriction in your lease agreement that states that only an agreed upon number of people can reside at that location?"

"Yes."

"So when the plaintiff started living at your house, what did you do?"

"I invited Mr. and Mrs. Farook for dinner to introduce them to my sister and get their permission."

Salman and Joseph looked at each other. Selma's statement was a surprise to them.

Foster continued with his questions. *"So did you notice anything unusual happening during dinner that bothered you?"*

"Yes, Mr. Farook was constantly gawking at my sister."

"How did that make her feel?"

"Objection your honor. How would this witness know the feelings of another person?" Sweeney interrupted.

"Sustained," the judge ruled.

"Mrs. Mendes, did your sister tell you later on how she felt?"

"Yes, when they left, she told me she felt uncomfortable. She was new in the country. She also knew that she was having dinner with the landlords and therefore was intimidated by them."

"So what happened a few days later?"

"A few days later Mr. Farook called and offered my sister a job."

"Did he ever offer you or any other member of your family, a job?"

"No, he didn't."

"No further questions," Mr. Foster finished.

"Cross examination, Miss Sweeney." The judge pointed towards the defense.

"Mrs. Mendes, how long have you known Mr. and Mrs. Farook?"

"About seven years."

"Have you always paid the rent on time?"

"Not always."

"Isn't it a fact that you have almost never paid the rent on time and you still owe Mr. Farook six thousand dollars?"

"May be. My husband pays all the bills."

"Isn't it a fact that this was not the first time the Farook's were invited to your house, but they have been there many times in the past?"

"Yes, but I had not seen this kind of behavior before."

"Isn't it a fact that Mr. Farook was not only lenient with his rent collection, but also helped you and your husband with business?"

"I don't know anything about the business."

"Isn't it also true that he was being good to you, way before Sophia even showed up?"

"Yes".

"No more questions for this witness Your Honor." Sweeney was done with Selma.

"Call your first witness, Miss Sweeney." The judge points towards the defense table.

"The defense calls Mr. Chanchai."

"Mr. Chanchai, for the record please tell the court your full name and how you know Mr. Farook."

"My name is Supot Chanchai. I own a Thai restaurant and Mr. Farook is my customer for many years."

"Mr. Chanchai, how big is your restaurant? Would you say you recognize most of your regular customers?"

"It's small. It accommodates about forty people. Yes, I recognize my regular customers."

"Do you recognize anyone near the plaintiffs and the defense tables?"

"Yes I recognize that lady," pointing towards Sophia, *"and that man,"* pointing towards Jose. *"They used to come with Mr. Farook. But I have not seen them for a few months."*

"Mr. Chanchai, do you remember if they consumed alcohol while they were at your establishment?"

"To the best of my recollection very little, maybe one or two drinks. Sometimes a small bottle of wine."

"When you say, a small bottle, what do you mean? How many glasses can be served from a small bottle?"

"It's about 20 oz., so if two people get a 20 oz. bottle, each can have no more than 2 glasses."

"Mr. Chanchai, you probably have people coming in and out of your establishment all the time, but did you ever see Mr. Farook having too much to drink? Did you ever see him intoxicated?"

"No, I have never seen him that way."

"Thank you, Mr. Chanchai. No further questions."

"You may now cross examine the witness Mr. Foster." The judge allowed.

"Mr. Chanchai, I want to remind you that you are under oath, and accuracy of your testimony is important. Do you really want us to believe that you know how many glasses of wine each of your customers always drinks?"

"Not always."

"So when you stated, in response to Miss Sweeney's question, that Mr. Farooq takes one or two drinks, was that a guess?"

"Yes, I was guessing."

"You also don't know for sure how much other people at his table drank. Isn't that right, Mr. Chanchai?"

"I can't say with surety."

"No further question of this witness, Your Honor."

"Call your next witness Miss Sweeney."

"The defense calls Mr. Jose Lopez to the stand."

"Mr. Lopez, please state your full name and tell the court your relationship to Mr. Farook."

"My name is Jose Lopez, and I work for Mr. Farook. He is my boss."

"How long have you worked for Mr. Farook?"

"About seven years."

"Can you describe for the court what your job duties are? What does it entail in a few sentences?"

"Mr. Farook has eight rental properties. I manage them, and I collect rent. I pay all the bills and take care of the paperwork."

"Is Mr. Farook a good boss?"

"Objection your honor, what is Mr. Lopez supposed to say? His boss is sitting in the court room, is he going to say he's a bad boss?"

"Overruled," the judge said, "you can answer the question Mr. Lopez."

"Yes, he is a good boss."

"Do all the tenants pay their rent on time?"

"Most of them do, a few don't."

"So when a tenant is unable to pay the rent, how does Mr. Farook deal with those tenants? Does he try to work with them or start the proceedings right away to kick them out?"

"He tries to work with them."

"When Miss Sophia Delgado started working with you, did Mr. Farook ask you to train her? Be gentle with her? Did he tell you she was new in the country, and therefore may not know much of anything?"

"Yes"

"Approximately how long do you think it took for Miss Delgado to start becoming productive?"

"About six months."

"So, would you agree that Mr. Farook was nice enough to pay her month after month to help her out?"

"Yes."

"Did Mr. Farook occasionally take both of you out for lunch?"

"Yes."

"I am sure there weren't any fixed days to go out, but approximately, how often do you think he would take you out?"

"Maybe once a month, sometimes more."

"So if we were to take a conservative estimate, and use your once a month scenario, it would be at least twenty four times in the last two years, since Miss Delgado worked there. Right?"

"Yes"

"Mr. Lopez, how long were your normal everyday lunch periods?"

"One hour."

"And how long were the lunches when you went out together with Mr. Farook?"

"About two hours."

"Two hours is a long period of time. Did you always talk business during lunch or did the discussions go to other areas as well?"

"We talked about business as well as other things, like sports, politics and what not. All three of us came from different countries, so we talked about back home, families, things like that."

"How about jokes, did you tell each other jokes?"

"Sometimes."

"What types of jokes were they? Were there adult jokes sometimes?"

"Yes."

"No further questions for this witnesses, Your Honor."

"Mr. Foster, cross examination."

"Mr. Lopez, before Miss Delgado started working with you, how often did Mr. Farook come to the office?"

"Once or twice a week."

"What about after she started working there?"

"Same. Once or twice a week."

"Mr. Lopez, I want to remind you, you're under oath. Did his pattern change?"

"Objection, your honor. Witness has already answered the question. He is being badgered."

"Overruled. Answer the question, Mr. Lopez."

"He still came once or twice, but started coming more frequently towards the end."

"Mr. Lopez, isn't it a fact that, even when he was not in the office, he always kept a close tab on you? In other words, he always knew where you were?"

"Yes."

"So, he always knew when you were not in the office?"

91

"Yes."

"Isn't it also a fact that Mr. Farook started to take Miss Delgado for lunch without you?"

"Only when I wasn't there."

"One last question, Mr. Lopez, have you ever seen Mr. Farook with other women?"

"Yes."

"No further questions for this witness your honor."

At the end of the first day, the judge adjourned the court for the weekend, with the order to reconvene on Monday.

Sophia had planned to spend the weekend with Foster. Jose had some catching up to do at the office. Salman and Sweeney decided to meet on Saturday to do some more prepping.

"How are you holding up?" Foster asked Sophia in the car while driving.

"I have a severe headache. I didn't realize it was going to be this hard. I wanted to punch that bitch in the face."

Foster found that amusing. *"Oh my goodness, I haven't seen this side of you. So you do get angry sometimes? I only see your smiling face all the time."*

"It's not funny John. Did you hear the things she was saying about me?"

"She was just doing her job. All lawyers do that. She wants to get you rattled, so the jury can see that. Remember what I told you, those twelve people are constantly watching you very carefully. They are watching yours and Salman's every move, and every reaction to the statements being made. You did very well today. Remember, it's going to be much harder when Joseph goes up there and when Salman goes up there. The worst will be when Sweeney puts you up there. Believe me, she will try to rip you apart. Unless you really want to go through this, let me know and we can still pull out. It's just that if we pull out, they win and we lose."

"No, no. I want to go forward. I don't want to lose to that man. I want to see him go to jail so bad, I will do anything."

"That's my girl." Foster was happy to hear that. He kept one hand on the wheel and playfully pulled Sophia towards him with the other.

"John, you are so good. You are so different in the courtroom than when you are with me. I'm so proud of you."

Foster loved hearing that from his sweetheart.

Selma and Joseph were mostly silent until they got home. They updated their son Danny, who wanted to know what happened in the court. When they got to their bedroom Selma begged Joseph to go easy on her sister. *"Please Joseph, she is my only sister. How can you do this to me? You are my husband, we are supposed to be on the same side."*

"What do you want me to do, lie for her? I have to tell the truth. I shouldn't have listened to you in the first place. She has been nothing but trouble ever since she got here. Our life was peaceful, we never used to fight. We worked together towards solving all problems. Look at us now, fighting all the time. Salman did so much for us, and now she is hell-bent on sending him to jail. Just because he is of a certain religion. The people who did bad things to her are Syrians, why does she want revenge from this guy? He is not only a non-Syrian but not even from the Middle East. On top of that this guy is not even religious. He doesn't pray, he drinks, cheats on his wife. I will never figure out your sister. The more I think about it, the more upset I get. I don't want to talk about it anymore. I have to get up early to go to work."

***

Jose was surprised to see Salman at the office on a Saturday.

"Jose, I want to ask you something. Why did you say that you have seen me with other women?"

Jose was nervous, but he pulled himself together, *"But I was being truthful."*

"I am not asking you to lie, but when have you seen me with other women?"

"A couple of times, few years back, but not recently."

"How do you know who they were? They could have been my sisters, my relatives, friends. Right?"

"Yes, you are right."

"I know I am right, damn it. You gave them the impression that I am a bloody womanizer."

"I am really sorry, I wasn't thinking."

"You know, my wife was sitting in the court room. I wonder what's going through her mind. My God, Jose, you are such an idiot."

The same afternoon Salman had a meeting with Sweeney in her office.

"So how are you holding up Mr. Farook? How do you feel the trial is going so far?"

Salman wasn't happy, but wasn't going to complain. Especially when it wasn't going to do any good. *"What can I say? I don't have a choice but to go through this. I'm counting on you, Nancy, to get me out of this mess. I have never felt so ashamed and helpless. I am the subject of ridicule in front of my wife and the whole world. It's unbelievable. How can the world be so unforgiving? One mistake and I see my whole world crumbling right in front of my eyes. So what do YOU think Nancy? How are things going so far, in your opinion? You think you will be able to sway the jurors to see our side?"*

"Well, I think it's still too early. A lot will depend on how Sophia handles herself on the stand and if she cracks under my questioning. Believe me, I am not going to be easy on her. She won't be able to charm me. I don't care how much Foster prepares her. By the way, Foster turned out to be a better

lawyer than I expected, he is good. And the fact that Joseph is on our side helps us a lot."

"Now I need to prepare you, some more, for your turn on the stand. You must remember that Foster wants to crack you, just as much as I will try to crack Sophia. He will throw every brick at you that he can think of. Every slam, every insult he can think of, to rattle you. You must not lose your cool, just let it slide. You cannot afford to let the jury think that you have a temper. Don't forget all twelve of them are keenly watching your every move. They are the jury and the judges. Hopefully they understand that they have a very big responsibility on their shoulders."

"I will do my best to control myself".

Monday morning arrived and the trial resumed as scheduled.

"Call your next witness, Miss Sweeney." Judge Malcolm pointed towards the defense table.

"We call Joseph Mendes to the witness stand."

Just like Selma, this was also Joseph's first experience. He was determined to tell the truth, even when Selma begged him to help her sister. He had always suspected Sophia's honesty and felt that Salman was being railroaded by her.

"Mr. Mendes, please state your full name and your relationships with the defendant and the plaintiff."

"My name is Joseph Mendes. Mr. Farook is my landlord and Miss Delgado is my wife's sister."

"Mr. Mendes, why are you a witness for Mr. Farook who is a defendant and not for your sister-in-law, who calls herself a victim?"

"Because I want to be on the side where I believe the truth is."

"Thank you sir. Can you tell the court how long have you lived in the United States?"

"Approximately seven years."

"How long have you known the plaintiff?"

"I have been married to her sister for twenty-seven years, so I have known her since then."

"What sort of relationship did you have with her, in all those years? Did you get along well? Were you cordial with each other or was it tense and distant?"

"It was cordial. She got married a few years after we did. We were invited to her in-laws sometimes and we invited them. It was normal."

"When you were invited to her in-laws, were there other people also present or just your two families?"

"Usually there were big parties where twenty to thirty other families were invited."

"During those parties how did the plaintiff behave? Was she friendly to everyone?"

"Yeah she was friendly, maybe too friendly sometimes."

"What do mean too friendly?"

"Sometimes she would get too flirtatious for my taste."

"Objection your honor, witness is expressing his opinion, instead of sticking to the facts," Foster interrupted.

"Sustained. Mr. Mendes, just state the facts."

"Did you help her in coming to the United States?"

"Yes. Because she's very close to my wife."

"Did you also help her get a job?"

"No, it was Mr. Farook's goodwill gesture to help her out."

"Has Mr. Farook asked you to testify on his behalf today?"

"No, he has not."

"No further questions of this witness, Your Honor."

"Mr. Foster, cross examination."

"Mr. Mendes isn't it a fact that you owe Mr. Farook six thousand dollars, and that's why you're testifying for him today?"

"I owe him the money, but that's not why I am testifying."

"Isn't it true that he offered to forgive your debt if you could talk Miss Delgado into dropping the charges?"

"I never talked to her about dropping anything."

"But you had your wife talk to her, didn't you?"

"No, I didn't tell my wife to talk to her either. She did it on her own."

"Aren't you testifying against her today, because you are upset that she didn't drop the charges?"

"I am upset because I believe whatever happened was consensual, and she is unappreciative of the man who tried to help her."

"Mr. Mendes, this is a court of law, only facts matter here, not your opinions."

"Objection Your Honor, defense is badgering the witness."

"Sustained. Mr. Foster, please refrain."

"Your Honor, I apologize, no further questions for this witness."

"Miss Sweeney, call your next witness."

"Your Honor, defense calls the defendant Mr. Farook."

Salman was more nervous than he had ever been. He was literally quivering when he got up to the stand. He looked up his wife who gave him a supportive look. He knew he was about to go on stage where the stakes had never been higher.

"Mr. Farook, please state your full name for the record."

"Salman Farook."

"Mr. Farook how long have you lived in the United States?"

"45 years."

"Were you in your teens when you came?"

"Yes, I was in my teens and came as a student."

"When you came to the US, did you have any relative, any friend who could guide you, help you?"

"No, I went to school in the day time and worked part time at night to support myself."

"Mr. Farook, how many children and grandchildren do you have?"

"I have two children and three grandchildren."

"Mr. Farook, other than the rental properties, do you have other businesses?"

"No, just the rental properties."

"Do all your rental lease agreements have a provision as to how many people can occupy the property? And if there is such a provision, is it strictly followed?"

"The provision is there but it is never strictly followed."

"Do all leases have the provision that the rent is due the first of the month, and is that strictly followed?"

"The provision is there but is not strictly followed."

"Mr. Joseph Mendes told this court in his testimony that he has been renting one of your properties for about seven years. In those years, approximately how many times did he not pay the rent on the first?"

"I don't know the exact count, but many times. I didn't mind because I considered him a friend and I certainly didn't care if he had more people living at the property than the lease allowed."

"Would it be fair to say that you were helping him, much earlier than when you ever saw Sophia Delgado?"

"Yes, from the first year he rented from me."

"What precipitated your offering a job to Miss Delgado?"

"I was new in the United States myself at one time, and no one helped me. I know how it feels to be a newcomer and I wanted to help."

"How long did she work there before the incident happened?"

"I believe about two years."

"Mr. Farook, in those two years, when the three of you worked together, did the working environment get casual? Did all of you talk about everything, or were some subjects taboo and to be avoided?"

"We talked about everything in a casual and friendly environment. We told jokes to each other, teased each other and had fun, while also getting the job done."

"Did those jokes get a little raunchy sometimes?"

"Sometimes."

"Did the environment include being touchy-feely?"

"Sometimes without doing it consciously."

"Did Miss Delgado mention being attracted to older men and that she found them to be more mature and sophisticated than men her own age?"

"Yes, more than once."

"Did she enjoy and look forward to the once a month luncheon?"

"Very much so."

"Your honor, no further questions."

"Mr. Foster, you may now cross examine the defendant."

"Mr. Farook, you testified earlier that when you first came to the United States you came as a student. You also said that you were supporting yourself by working part time at night. Students coming to this country aren't allowed to work, by law. Did you not know that?"

"No, I didn't know that."

"So you were breaking the laws of this country from the very beginning."

"Objection, your honor, we are not here to discuss immigration matters, that happened fifty years ago," Sweeney objected.

"Your Honor, I am trying to establish a fact that the defendant ignored the laws of this land even back then," Foster countered.

"Your Honor, I am sure we have all driven our cars more than 55 miles an hour sometimes, and that's breaking the law too." Sweeney wasn't going to back down.

"Mr. Foster, just move on," Judge Malcolm directed.

"Mr. Farook, you testified in one of your answers to Miss Sweeney, that you always liked to help newcomers to the U.S. Can you please tell the court how many other people you helped before Miss Delgado?"

"I don't remember. I don't keep count."

"Ten, five, three?"

"I don't remember."

"You don't remember helping a single person?"

"Objection, your honor, witness has already answered the question."

99

"Sustained. Ask your next question Mr. Foster."

"Mr. Farook, you said in your testimony that adult jokes were told in the office, did Miss Delgado ever tell a joke?"

"No, but she seemed to always enjoy them."

"Mr. Farook, in his testimony, Mr. Jose Lopez stated that he has seen you with other women. Did you bring other women to the office to sleep with?"

"I have never slept with anybody but my wife."

"Objection your honor, defense requests that answer be stricken from the records, it's irrelevant to this case."

"Sustained. Ask your next question, Mr. Foster."

"Is it fair to say you constantly stayed in touch with Mr. Jose Lopez through phone calls and texts?"

"Of course, he is the office manager and I have to give him instructions."

"So wasn't it convenient for you to send him away to do outside work so that you could be alone with Miss Delgado and take her out for lunch?"

"I did not do that."

"Mr. Farook, you were planning this for a long time, weren't you? You were going to wait for Mr. Lopez to be away. Then you would take Miss Delgado out for lunch, get her drunk and take advantage of her vulnerability."

"No, I did not plan any such thing. We were both equal participants. It was consensual, and it was totally impulsive."

"Mr. Farook, did you hear Miss Delgado asking you to stop repeatedly."

"But I knew she didn't mean it. She was giving encouraging signals for a long time."

"No further questions for the defendant, Your Honor."

"Mr. Foster, is the plaintiff ready to go to the witness stand"?
"Yes, Your Honor."
"We call the plaintiff Miss Delgado to the stand."

Sophia was extremely nervous, but she knew she had the advantage of being questioned by John, to start with.

"Miss Delgado, please state your full name for the record."

"Sophia Delgado."

"Miss Delgado, please tell the court under what circumstances you came to the United States and from which country?"

"I came to America from Syria. Both my parents died in a car accident about fifteen years ago. My husband was killed in a suicide bomb blast five years ago. I was only left with my teenage daughter and they also killed her two and half years ago."

"What do you mean by they? Who are you referring to?"

"ISIS jihadi savages killed my beautiful, sweet, little, innocent baby." With that Sophia started sobbing uncontrollably.

The judge ordered a break in the proceedings until she calmed down. When the break was over Foster continued questioning Sophia.

"I am very sorry Miss Delgado that you have to answer these questions. Do you have any idea why those people would target an innocent little girl?"

"My child went to a Catholic school, and they targeted that school bus. The bus was full of non-Muslim children. In their twisted minds, it's okay for them to kill all non-Muslims, who they call infidels, and also their children."

"Is that why you came to United States? Because you became isolated or because it was no longer safe to stay there?"

"Both. My only living family member, my sister, was in California. I wanted to join her and start a new life, if possible."

"When Mr. Farook offered you a job, were you surprised, and did you accept it right away?"

"I was surprised. Both my sister and I were skeptical at first. We were wondering why he was doing that. I didn't know anything, and I was not familiar with the American system at all. But I needed a job and I had to learn everything quickly."

"Miss Delgado, when you started working there, when did you start noticing some changes?"

"Objection your honor, leading the witness."

"Sustained. Rephrase your question, Mr. Foster."

"So did you notice anything different from the time you started till the end?"

"Yes, at first Mr. Farook used to come once in a while to the office, but then started to come very frequently. Often he would give Jose some outside assignment."

"Mr. Farook has testified that there were jokes being told in the office. Did all three of you tell jokes to each other?"

"No, only the boss told the jokes, and the employees listened and politely smiled."

"Miss Delgado, did you ever encourage Mr. Farook to think that you were interested in him romantically, in any way shape or form?"

"No, he is a married man and my boss. I have met his wife and I like her very much. I would never try to break someone's marriage."

"When you went for lunch, did you always order drinks with the meal?"

"No, I never had a drink at lunch, except for one time, the day of the incident."

"Miss Delgado, on the day of the incident, how many drinks did you have?"

"Between the two of us, we finished a whole bottle of wine."

"Miss Delgado, do you remember anything specific that the defendant said on that day?"

"Yes, he said, 'I wanted you since the first time I laid my eyes on you.'"

"Miss Delgado, did you try to stop Mr. Farook's advancements?"

"Yes, but he kept saying it's okay, it's okay. He didn't stop."

"No further questions, Your Honor."

"Miss Sweeney, you may now cross examine the plaintiff."

"Miss Delgado, is Mr. Foster your current boyfriend?"

"Objection your honor. Totally irrelevant and inappropriate." Foster jumped up with the objection.

"Sustained. Miss Sweeney, please refrain."

"Miss Delgado, isn't it a fact that Mr. Farook repeatedly told you that he was helping you because nobody helped him, and he knows how a newcomer feels?"

"Yes."

"Isn't it a fact that he didn't change his schedule for a long time after you started working there, and sometimes he had to change his schedule to catch up with his books?"

"I don't know anything about that."

"Did you not tell Mr. Farook that you prefer older men and not men your own age? Did you not tell him that older men are more mature and sophisticated?"

"I was talking about my late husband."

"Do you blame Mr. Farook in any way for what happened to your late husband and your daughter on religious grounds?"

"No."

"Are you sure?"

"Objection, your honor, witness has already answered the question."

"Sustained, move on Miss Sweeney."

"Miss Delgado, isn't it a fact that you never asked Mr. Farook to stop at any point?"

"No, I asked him to stop."

"At what point did you ask him to stop?"

"When he started kissing me and removing my clothes."

"So, he removed your clothes forcibly?"

"Yes."

"Did you try to run away from him?"

"Yes, I did."

"So, he forcibly pinned you down, so that you couldn't run away?"

"Yes."
"I don't believe you, remember you're under oath."
"Objection your honor, defense is badgering the witness."
"Sustained, Miss Sweeney, ask your next question."
"Are you willing to take a polygraph?"
"Yes."
"Defense rests, your honor."

13

"Mr. Foster, please make your closing statement."

"Ladies and Gentlemen, in front of you is the case of a woman who has suffered tragedies of epic proportions. The evidence, we believe, leads to the inescapable conclusion that the defendant raped Miss Sophia Delgado. This was far from being an impulsive occurrence. This was well-planned, a designed, well thought out and calculated action on the defendant's part. We strongly believe that the defendant made a decision, the minute he first laid his eyes on her, that he wanted her. He himself said so, to the victim. The truth came out during his unconscionable behavior. He came up with the excuse that he likes to help newcomers to the United States. When asked how many other people he had helped, he couldn't come up with a single name.

The defendant tried every which way to get Miss Delgado to drop the charges. He offered her money. He offered her sister and brother-in-law money. He even contacted me and tried to threaten me personally. In all my years of practice, I have never been threatened by a defendant. He has shown total disregard for the law from the time he came to the United States.

He tried to mislead the jury that there were tawdry jokes flying around in the office, but contrary to his assertions, it was only him telling the jokes. His own office manager testified that there were other women involved with the defendant.

Ladies and Gentlemen, he was waiting for the right opportunity to make his move. He went for it when the opportunity presented itself and attacked like an animal waiting for its prey."

"Miss Sweeney, your closing statement."

"Ladies and Gentlemen, you have a very difficult task and a very heavy responsibility ahead of you, to see through this mirage. Please do not fall into this false image being created, that the plaintiff is this poor innocent woman. She knew exactly what she was doing. The defendant is, by nature, a helping individual. He helped this Syrian immigrant family way before he knew that Miss Delgado existed. This family owed him thousands of dollars before he knew that Miss Delgado existed.

He helped this family with setting up their business endeavors, before he knew that Miss Delgado existed. Her own brother-in-law acknowledged all this. Miss Delgado is a beautiful woman and she knows it. She also knows how to take advantage of that, and enjoys being flirtatious. Her own brother-in-law, who has known her for decades, has seen her in action at the parties.

We acknowledge that she has gone through some rough times but it has nothing to do with the defendant. We also believe that Miss Delgado has this convoluted thinking process that equates the current chaos in the Middle East to all Muslims. She does not want to accept the fact that the defendant has nothing to do with the Middle East. She seems to believe that since the majority of people in the Middle East countries, and a majority of people of Pakistan, have a common religion, they are all the same. There should be no doubt that Miss Delgado was giving encouraging signals to the defendant all the time. She enjoyed going for lunches. She had preferences of restaurants to go to. One time things did go further than usual, but it was only because both parties didn't stop, not just the defendant. She is blaming all of this on the defendant. We believe she is doing this for two reasons. One, she is remorseful for her participation in that incident; second, it probably gives her some satisfaction to blame it on a guy whose religious beliefs she abhors.

Ladies and Gentlemen, as I indicated earlier in my statement, you have a heavy burden on your shoulders. We urge you to please look at this man's life time record, a self-made man, a hard working individual coming from a backward *country. A family man who always had a clean record, raised a family of successful professional children. Now the judgment is in your hands. The right decision would be to see what two consenting adults decided to do one afternoon. The wrong decision could destroy an innocent man's life, and let the other equal participant go scot-free.*

"Rebuttal Mr. Foster"

"Ladies and Gentlemen, Miss Sophia Delgado has gone through enough tragedies in her life. She wants to make sure that the defendant doesn't take advantage of any other woman. The defense would like to make this case into a "he-said, she-said" case, but clearly that's not what this case is about. The evidence is clear that the defendant's testimony is not trust worthy and cannot be believed for the following reasons:

1. *He has deliberately ignored the laws of the United States from the time he came.*
2. *He said he likes to help new comers, but couldn't come up with a single example.*
3. *He tried to give an impression that all three of them told tawdry jokes, but he was the only one who told the jokes.*
4. *He tried to give an impression that he doesn't cheat on his wife but evidence showed otherwise.*
5. *He waited for his office manager to be away and as soon as he got the opportunity he attacked the victim.*
6. *He admitted to the victim that he wanted her since the first time he laid eyes on her.*
7. *He lied that his actions were impulsive and he didn't plan anything. The fact of the matter is that he had brought condoms with him that day. The victim saw them after the act. If it was impulsive and he didn't know what was going to happen, then why did he bring condoms?*
8. *He called me personally and threatened me.*

Finally, ladies and gentlemen, I would like to emphasize that even if we were to believe each and everything that the defendant and his attorney has testified to, you should still find him guilty for the following reason:

In answer to my question, why didn't he stop when Miss Delgado was asking him to stop, his response was, "She didn't mean it for me to stop." In other words, he heard her asking him to stop. He just assumed that she didn't mean it.

Ladies and gentlemen of the jury the law is very clear on this subject, and each one of you are obligated and duty bound to follow the law. The law states: "A participant in sexual activity has the option to withdraw consent at any time. The withdrawal of that consent puts the burden on the other party to stop immediately. Continuing after consent has been withdrawn would fall under the definition of rape."

After the closing arguments and summations had been made, the judge ordered the jury to go to the deliberation room after giving them the final jury instructions.

After only three hours the jury came back with the verdict.

"We the jury, in the case of Sophia Delgado vs Salman Farook find the defendant guilty."

Salman and his attorney were stunned. Salman's face was full of emotions. He was shaking his head sideways with an incredulous look at having been found guilty. His lawyer apologized profusely and promised him that she would appeal. His wife, Zainub, cried watching her larger than life husband being handcuffed and taken away by the Sheriffs. As he was being taken away, Salman looked at her apologetically, asking for her forgiveness with a silent stare. His eyes said to her, *"what a mess I have created for myself and dragged you into it".*

At the sentence hearing Salman was sentenced to six years in prison.

14

Within two months Sophia gave up her apartment and moved in with Foster. She was now a resident of the posh Newport Beach community. Foster proudly introduced his trophy girlfriend to his inner circle. Both of Foster's adult children lived in other states. His thirty-two-year-old married daughter, Debbie, lived in Virginia, while his thirty-four-year-old, single son, Michael, lived in New York. She hadn't met either one yet. Sophia was enjoying her new friends and neighbors.

She started going to a nearby gym with a neighbor friend. And after a month of living in her new home she invited Selma to visit her.

"When are you going to come visit me Selma? You haven't even seen this house. You don't even know where I live."

"You know how it is with Joseph. He is still upset at both of us."

"But you must come. Just come by yourself if he doesn't want to come."

"Oh, I know for sure he is not going to, but I will come soon."

When Selma finally got to see the humongous house her sister was living in, right next to the beach, she just couldn't help thinking how lucky she was. She also knew that the word lucky was forbidden in her sister's presence and therefore wouldn't dare say it. She just admired and told her how happy she was for her and she deserved all the happiness. Both sisters couldn't help comparing the life in the United States versus life in Syria and shook their heads realizing how God worked in mysterious ways.

Sophia wanted to meet Foster's son and daughter and had expressed interest several times, but Foster didn't seem quite as enthusiastic about the idea. He kept telling her that he had told them about her on the phone.

She finally met them during the Thanksgiving holidays, eight months after moving in with their father. She then realized why Foster had been so reluctant. They didn't approve of their dad being with a woman so much younger. They were both rude when Foster wasn't around. The son even told her that she should be with somebody his age not his dad's age. It was hard, but she knew how to handle this kind of stuff. She had seen worse. She didn't mention this to Foster. She figured they were only visiting for a few days, and she didn't want to create a rift.

After having lived with Foster for two years, Sophia felt quite adjusted to the new life. She had been granted the United States citizenship on a fast track basis, thanks to her lawyer-boyfriend John. She rarely thought about Syria. She wasn't even interested in watching any news about Syria. She had heard from Andrew a couple of times. One time he informed her about his mother's deteriorating health, and soon after, about her passing. Her contacts with Selma had also gone down, mostly because of Joseph.

Selma had told Sophia in her last conversation that Joseph's business had picked up quite a bit and they had even hired a couple of people. They had paid off all their debt and Danny had gone back to school, restarting where he had left off.

15

In one of their many conversations, Selma had mentioned that there was an organization by the name of SCO, Syrian Christian Organization, in California that she had recently found out about. This organization attracted expatriates from Syria who had settled in the U.S. They organized different cultural events, parties and what not, for people from back home.

"Well they are having this party in early December, and Joseph as usual, is not interested. Would you like to go with me?" Selma sounded excited.

"What is the party about, do you know?"

"They are calling it a Christmas party, although it's in early December."

"I would love to go. I will see if John wants to join us, if not, then just the two of us can go."

Sophia asked Foster if he would join her and Selma. Unfortunately, he was busy with an important case and would not be able to go. Sophia and Selma went without their men.

The party was lively and crowded. Most people seemed to be from the Middle East. The music as well as food was mixed, American and Middle Eastern. Drinks were flowing, the dance floor was packed. Sophia noticed that there were several couples at the table next to theirs. She also noticed a man sitting by himself. She told Selma to look in a subtle way. Selma thought he was extremely good looking. In the meantime, some old guy popped up from nowhere and asked Selma for a dance. She of course went. A few minutes later Sophia noticed the same man at the next table was looking at her. They both smiled. In the meantime, the music had stopped. Selma came back and started talking about the old guy she was dancing with, what good a dancer he was. Sophia was anxiously waiting for the music to start and hoping the guy from the next table would ask her for a dance. In the meantime, even without music, they were sneaking peaks at each other and smiling. Selma couldn't help noticing what was going on, she just smiled knowing her sister was up to her old tricks again.

The music started, and sure enough, the guy asked Sophia for a dance. Sophia was of course waiting. His tall, slender frame was encased in a modern black leather jacket. His dark eyes were gleaming. His charisma was oozing from every pore as he cracked a wry smile at Sophia. On the dance floor, he told her his name was Anthony Cruz. Since the music was so loud and they couldn't talk much, they kept looking at each other and smiling. Sophia didn't remember the last time, if ever, she had been mesmerized by a man like this. He was so charming.

"It's too loud here, I think we should get off the dance floor, and find a place to talk."

Sophia agreed. They didn't go back to their tables, but found another corner with only standing room to talk.

"I am so happy to meet you. You are so beautiful." He sounded genuine.

"You are not so bad yourself."

"So tell me about yourself. Where have you been hiding all my life?"

"You first," she said.

"Okay, I will go first. I am Tony. I was born in Lebanon. I am forty-five years old, my parents came to America when I was 10 years old. I am a software engineer working for a big corporation."

"Are you married?" Sophia interrupted.

"No, are you?"

"No."

"Boyfriend?"

"Yes."

"Then I will have to steal you from him."

They both laughed.

This was a new experience for Sophia. All her life she had been associated with older men, first Delgado and then Foster. She didn't even know how it felt to be with a man her own age. Although it had been just a few minutes since she met him, she already felt comfortable with him. She knew she was playing with fire and this was a very dangerous game. She also knew that although Foster was nice to her, he could be just the opposite when he needed to be. She had seen his anger and you didn't want to be near him when he was that way. But Tony's magnetism was working on her in a way that was beyond explanation. It was like he had put a magic spell on her.

Tony noticed the quietness in the air. With a smile he started waiving his hand near her face, *"Hello, hello? What happened to you? Looks like you dozed off with your eyes still open. You made me to tell you about myself, now it's your turn."*

Sophia knew it was her turn, but she kept staring at him and wouldn't say anything. Tony gave her a puzzled look. Then to his amazement she just ran into his arms and started sobbing. He was confused, yet wanted to help. Why was this beautiful woman crying? He wanted to know, yet he didn't want to pressure her into talking. He just tried to calm her down. *"It's okay, everything will be okay. Are you in some kind of trouble? Are you under any threat?"*

"No, no, I'm fine. I just got emotional for some reason. I will tell you about myself some other time, okay?"

Tony started joking with her. *"Oh, so there will be another time. I am so glad to hear that. I thought you wouldn't want to see me again because I make you cry."*

Sophia was smiling again, *"You don't make me cry, you make me laugh."*

"We better go back, my sister must be wondering where I am."

They exchanged information about each other on their cell phones. Tony wanted another hug before they parted, which Sophia was more than happy to give. Before he left, she introduced Tony to Selma, and then he took them to his table and introduced them to his friends. Since they were only two, it was easy to accommodate them. Some people sensed the romance in the air and they quickly switched their chairs around so Tony and Sophia could sit next to each other. Sophia didn't want the evening to end, but it did. Before leaving she asked Tony not to call her, and that she would call him. He understood.

On the way back, Selma was really angry with her.

"Do you have any idea what you are doing? Are you out of your mind? What is wrong with you?"

Sophia didn't remember her sister ever being so upset. She kept quiet.

"Look I have always been, and will always be, on your side, but Sophia what you are doing here is just beyond the pale. I don't even want to imagine what will happen if John finds out. It would be understandable if John was a jerk or treating you badly or something like that. But no, he is just the opposite. Look at the things he has done for you. He brought you here from the Syrian hellhole. He fought for you against that Pakistani guy you hated so much, because of his religion, and look at the castle you are living in now near the beach. How much more can a man do for you? And you are going to treat him this way?"

Selma could see tears forming in her sister's eyes, as she was driving.

"Look I didn't mean to upset you. All I can say is just think about it. Think about the consequences."

"Selma, my dear, dear sister, I love you from the bottom of my heart. You have done more for me than a parent would do for her child. I also know that I have hurt you at times. You have done things for me against your own wishes to accommodate me. Don't you think I know all that? I do. But, some things are just unexplainable, and what happened today, I can't explain. My brain and my heart are racing in opposite directions. I have never felt this way before in my life. I don't know what else to tell you. Let me tell you one more thing that I have never told

anyone before. Yes, Delgado and Foster have taken care of me and even loved me in their own ways, but I think a woman needs more. I didn't have that deep, way deep, connection with them and I miss that. I am not saying that I have that with Tony, because I just met him, but he did make me realize the missing part. I don't even know if all this is making any sense to you, or you think I am crazy."

"I have no doubt you are crazy," Selma said with a smile.

Sophia dropped her sister off and headed back to her own place. When she got home it was late, but Foster was still up working.

"Did you have a good time sweetheart? I was getting concerned. You never come home so late."

"Oh, I am fine. I had to drop off Selma."

"How was the party? I'm sorry I couldn't come with you. Did you make some new friends"?

"The party was good. Selma and I had a good time. We didn't know anybody there, so we just enjoyed the food and listened to the music."

"I am glad you both enjoyed yourselves. You should do that more often, have fun, enjoy life, meet new people."

Sophia smiled to herself thinking how ironic it was for him to say that.

"Oh Sophia, I wanted to let you know this case I am working on is a very complicated case. I will need to travel to New York in a couple of weeks. Since I will be there on Friday, Michael wants me to spend the weekend with him. So I will only be gone for three days. Will you be able to manage?"

"Oh yeah, I can manage. Remember I was living by myself before I moved here? I will be okay. I wish I could go with you though. Michael will probably want to spend time with you alone."

"I wish Michael and Debbie would have been more welcoming towards you, but what can I say? It is, what it is. I guess we can't have everything we want in life."

Sophia wasn't able to sleep all night. She couldn't get Tony out of her mind. She kept scolding herself by thinking, you are acting like a teenager, you are being stupid. How are you going to handle John's wrath if he finds out? Joseph is going to let Selma have it. I told you all along, your sister is no good. She persuaded John to put an innocent man in jail, who had been good to us and to her. All these thoughts just wouldn't stop.

The most she could control herself before calling Tony was three days. She had hardly slept for three days.

"Hello, how are you?" She tried to suppress her excitement.

"Where did you disappear? I was wondering if I would hear from you again."

"It's been only three days. You sound like I took three months to call you."

"The feelings you have left me with make three days seem like three months."

"Flattery is not going to get you anywhere, Mr. Cruz."

"Oh, you remember my last name. That's a good sign."

"I have a very good memory. I don't forget anything."

"So, when am I going to see you? You promised during your crying session you would tell me later. I don't know anything about you."

"Yeah, I cry a lot."

"Why?"

"You will find out some day."

"You like to keep people guessing don't you?"

"Maybe," she said with a laugh.

Two days later they met for lunch. They greeted each other with a big hug. Sophia was still confused and terrified of the possibility of being exposed. Yet, she was enthralled by these new found feelings. They found a corner table where they could talk to their heart's content. Tony was anxious to find out about this mysterious beauty. When she was finished telling her story, he was floored. He could barely speak. All his joviality was gone.

"I don't know if I have ever come across someone like you. How can God put one person through so much pain in one lifetime? You are a remarkable person, Sophia. I have so much admiration for you that words can't begin to describe."

"Okay, okay, that's enough. You want me to start crying again?" Sophia asked with a smile.

"Oh no, please don't. We are sitting in a restaurant, if people see you crying they might call the police on me, suspecting I am doing something to you," Tony said jokingly.

They talked more, asking each other questions.

"So how come you never got married?" Sophia asked.

"Well, I was waiting for you to become available." Tony tried to weasel out.

"But I am still not available, I have a boyfriend."

"Remember I told you, I am going to steal you from him."

"You can try but it's not going to be easy. He is a lawyer, he will put you in jail."

"I don't care if he is a lawyer or a judge, I am not like that idiot Pakistani. He won't be able to put me in jail. I know how to protect myself." Tony smiled.

After a while a silence came over them and they sat just staring at each other. Sophia broke the silence. *"So where do we go from here?"*

Neither one had an answer to that question. Sophia asked if he would like to visit her at the house when John was out of town. Tony told her to text him the address and the time to come.

Early Friday morning Foster left on his trip. Sophia dropped him off at the airport. He said he would call when he got to New York. On the way to the airport Foster picked up a little uneasiness on her part. He chalked it up to her anticipation of being alone in the house and being a little nervous. She was supposed to pick him up Sunday evening.

She had a few hours to get ready before Tony would arrive.

"Oh my God, this is where you live?" Tony was flabbergasted when he first saw the house. *"Goodness, this is like a dream house."*

Sophia had prepared some fish together with some salad. Tony was hungry after a long drive. Both enjoyed the meal. She poured some white wine that she knew Tony liked since she had seen him drinking white wine at the party. The evening couldn't have been more enjoyable for both of them. Throughout the evening she had these mixed feelings. She was scared, guilty, nervous and happy all at the same time. After the meal, Sophia thought it would be a great idea to watch the sunset from the balcony. In her excitement she forgot that the balcony was close to the bedroom. Too late. They watched the sunset. It was terrifically romantic. They both looked deep into each other's eyes. Sophia melted in his arms. Tony kissed her for the first time. She kissed him back. This was the point of no return for both. Now, neither one cared about where they were, whose house it was, anything. They could care less about the consequences of what they were about to do.

Sophia grabbed Tony's red silk necktie like a dog's leash, walked slowly backwards pulling it all along, and took him to the bedroom. Tony, like an obedient puppy, was letting her do whatever she wanted. They were both drunk, not with alcohol, but with uncontrollable desire.

When the time came for Tony to leave, it was unbearable for her. She just kept clinging on and wouldn't let go of him. It felt to her as if he was going away on some deployment or to some far away country when in reality he would be only a phone call away.

A new chapter had begun in Sophia's life following that weekend. She was terrified of the thought of John finding out.

On Sunday, as a dutiful girlfriend, she went to pick John up at the airport. *"How was your trip, John? How's Michael?"*

"I got a lot of work done. We made good progress on our case. Michael is fine, still ornery, wants everything his way. But overall, it was a good trip. How was your weekend"?

"Oh I didn't do much. Missed you a lot, watched some movies and that's about it."

Foster did notice the uneasiness and discomfort in her demeanor again, but not to the extent that he felt he needed to question it.

Although Foster was in his sixties, he was very conscientious of staying fit. Feeling lethargic and tired after a long flight, he decided to go for a run along the water. He asked Sophia if she wanted to come along. She didn't seem interested. He knew that running was not her thing. She did work out at the gym, but running was something she didn't care for.

John went alone. He ran into his neighbor Roger while running along the path, who was running in the opposite direction. He was a prolific runner who ran twice a day. They said hi to each other.

"Hi Roger, how have you been?"

"Good, John. Hey that was a nice sunset last night, yeah?"

"Oh was it? I missed it, I was out of town."

"Oh really, I could had sworn I saw two shadows on your balcony. Oh well, I was running and it was getting dark. I am delusional sometimes, don't mind me."

They said good bye and went their own ways in opposite directions.

John didn't know what to make of Roger's comment. On one hand, Roger did say it was getting dark and he was delusional sometimes, on the other hand, his balcony was so separate from other houses that it would be hard for someone to mix up the balconies. He also remembered her jitteriness to and from the airport. His initial instinct was to push aside these stupid thoughts thinking Sophia is such a nice, innocent woman. But his lawyer's instincts were telling him to be cautious. He decided not to mention anything to her about Roger's remarks. When he arrived back home after the run, Sophia was preparing a nice Italian dish for him, his favorite.

Foster was in love. This was the first time he had felt this way after his wife's death. Being a wealthy, successful lawyer there were plenty of fish in the pond. He knew there were plenty of bachelorettes available, but he found most of them to be plastic, needy and measured men by the weight of their pockets. Sophia was different. She was not only beautiful, she was not money hungry. Still he couldn't shake off his neighbor's comments from his thoughts. Although he trusted her, he didn't want to take any chances, yet he didn't do anything about it.

Sophia's contacts with Tony had become more frequent. Foster had worked long hours all his career, as most lawyers do. That was good for Sophia. Although she never dared to invite Tony to her place again, she frequently went to his posh condo. Tony's software engineering position gave him the option to work remotely from home, and he took full advantage.

16

Foster was beginning to notice Sophia's phone being busy more often. He also noticed her shopping habits had changed and she was going to the gym more often. Although these were minor shifts on their own, when combined it with his neighbor's comments, it brought him enough concern. He decided to do something about it to get a peace of mind.

He decided to hire a private investigator, Jim Benson. He had used this P.I. in the past for a client, but this time he needed his services for his own personal use. He didn't expect this P.I. to find anything about Sophia, but just to get rid of those nagging stupid thoughts, he decided to just go ahead with it.

Three weeks later he got a call from Benson. His secretary said it sounded urgent. *"What's up Jim"?*

"John, I have some information for you that you're not going to like."

"What do you mean?"

"Well, she's been seeing a guy. He looks Middle Eastern, fortyish, lives in a condo near Santa Monica. I have some photos of them in a restaurant."

"How soon can you get to my office?"

"About forty minutes."

"Ok, I will wait for you."

Foster's head was spinning. He didn't know what to do, who to call. The first thing he did was to call his secretary in the lobby, telling her to cancel all his afternoon appointments due to an emergency. He didn't want to take any action before he saw the photos with his own eyes.

Benson came in with an envelope in his hands. He immediately handed the envelope to Foster. Foster tore it open and couldn't believe his eyes. Benson had taken about a dozen pictures that left no doubt that these two were not just friends. One picture showed them kissing.

"Wow, how I could be such a fool?" Foster was seething with anger. *"I will never trust another human being on this earth again."* Trying to control himself, he realized Benson was sitting in front of him. He thanked Benson for the good job and told him he would get in touch with him soon.

Foster left the office with the envelope and headed home.

Sophia was sitting on the couch watching television, when he got home. He sat down next to her, putting the envelope on the side, picked up the remote control next to her and turned off the TV. She immediately leaned towards him to greet and kiss. He moved away from her, but still sat on the couch.

"Are you okay? What's the matter?" She asked, not knowing the contents of the envelope.

"Let me ask you something Sophia, do you care about me?"

"Of course. I love you. You are my heart and soul. You have given me a new life. Why do you ask?"

"Okay, let me ask you another question. Will you ever cheat on the person who gave you a new life?"

"No, of course not. But why are you asking these silly questions?"

"Let me ask you one more question. When I was in New York, did you have a visitor here?"

Sophia was shocked, her face turned pale. She was trembling with fear. She couldn't even look up to make eye contact. She kept quiet, looking down at the floor. He picked up the envelope, opened it and threw all the pictures at her. The pictures scattered all around her, some face up others face down. She could see the content of the pictures that fell near her with face up.

"You whore! You dirty fucking Arab! I give you everything, and you have the nerve to bring your lover to fuck you in my house, in my bed. I want you to get the fuck out of my house."

"John, I am really sorry. I am really sorry. Please let me explain."

"No, I will never forgive you".

"John, please," Sophia begged crying hysterically.

"How can I have been so naive? You are such a good actress. I had no clue what was going on behind my back. How long have you been carrying on these shenanigans?"

"I met him three weeks ago, and believe me, it happened only once."

"You think I am going to believe anything that comes out of your mouth?"

"I swear. You can ask my sister, we were together when I met him."

"I have nothing to do with your whole goddamn family. I have done enough for you people. You are all back stabbers. Users. No more favors."

"John, please, my sister is not like that."

"Save your breath, you just told me she was with you, so obviously she knew what was going on."

"No, no she tried her best to stop me from getting involved with another man."

"You are a liar, everything that comes out of your mouth is a lie. Now, I feel sorry for that poor Pakistani fellow, rotting in jail because of your lies."

"John I am begging you, please don't be like that."

"I just want you to make arrangements and get the fuck out. That's all I have to say. Maybe the lover boy can help you move."

Sophia was now faced with another blow in her life. Although she had faced severe blows in the past, one can never get used to the severity. Each one stings at different levels.

***

The next day after Foster left for work, she called Tony, crying hysterically. She was crying so hard that she was incoherent. All he gathered was that she needed help. Finally, she calmed down.

"Foster somehow found out that you were here."

"How? Maybe he has hidden cameras installed?"

"I don't know, but he wants me out of his house. I will have to find a place quickly. I don't know what to do."

"Don't worry Sophia, maybe this is a blessing in disguise. You can move in with me. This is a small place as compared to the castle you are used to," Tony said jokingly.

Sophia was in no joking mood, but what she heard brought euphoria in her voice. *"Really Tony, oh my goodness, are you serious? I have seen your place, I would be okay with half that size, as long as I have you."*

"Well, it's settled then, start packing. I will call in sick. How long will it take for you to pack?"

"You know, I am just going to take the essentials. I want to be out of here today. Give me about four hours."

"Okay, I will rent a truck. Try to be ready by three."

"Okay."

Tony emptied a few areas for Sophia before he went to pick her up. Sophia already had the experience of being in a cramped place while living with Selma. She was just too excited at the prospect of being with Tony. The first thing she did after moving in was to call Selma. She knew that if she didn't tell her right away, there would be a hell to pay.

"Guess where I am calling you from?" Sophia wanted to surprise Selma.

"I don't know. Why are you always playing games with me? What are you up to this time?"

"I am calling you from Tony's place."

"Do you want to give me a heart attack? Are you out of your mind? What if Foster finds out?"

"Selma calm down. He already found out, and he asked me to move out."

"Oh my goodness, how did he find out?"

"You know he was out of town so I invited Tony over. I think he has hidden cameras in the house. I didn't even know where they were."

"Wow, these lawyers are so clever. So how did he react when he first found out? How angry was he? He didn't try to hit you or anything did he?"

"No, but you won't believe the things he said. He called me a dirty Arab, a whore, and everything else he could think of. The blood was coming out of his eyes. I had never seen him like that. Can you believe it? After three years, now I am a dirty Arab. I'm kind of glad I found out what he REALLY thinks of me. After all, I am not his wife, I can see anyone I want. Right?"

"Come on Sophia, you made him angry. I am not surprised. Anyways how did you move so fast?"

"I just grabbed the few things I really wanted. Tony's place is not that big. I didn't take any of the things that Foster gave me, he can keep them."

"I can't believe how fast things can change. My God, I don't know how you manage Sophia, you are so brave. I certainly couldn't do it. Maybe you should write a book about your life. I bet you it would be a best seller."

"I don't know about that, but one thing for sure, it's been eventful."

"I just hope you finally get the happiness with Tony you deserve."

"Selma, I really think this is it for me. I have finally found my soulmate. It has been a long journey but now I'm happy. I enjoy every minute I am with him, and would you believe I will be with him twenty-four hours a day."

"I am so happy to hear my little sister talk like that. I wish I could share this news with Joseph, but I can't."

"Is he still mad at me?" Tell him to get over it, it's been almost three years."

"He still talks about Salman. I know if he finds out about this, he will take Foster's side. I am glad I haven't told him anything about Tony. He would bite my ears off with taunts, if he found out."

By the time Foster got home, she was gone. He was surprised she moved out so quickly. In a way, he was glad that it ended smoothly without any incidents. He was so disgusted by the whole thing that he never wanted to see her face again. He called his son and daughter to let them know what happened. They were nice enough not to embarrass their dad with the we told you so words.

Two months went by. Sophia was so happy to be with Tony that she didn't miss the beach house for too long. She told him over and over again, how she thought they were made for each other. Although Tony worked mostly from home, he had to go to the office once or twice a week.

Sometimes Sophia wondered how little she knew about Tony. But she figured he would tell her whenever he wanted, so what's the rush. Subconsciously she also didn't want anything to change. Everything was so perfect, she was with someone she adored, she was living in the best country in the world, and they had a good comfortable life. What else could a person ask for?

In spite of two months passing by, Foster was still feeling the sting of the deceit he'd been a victim of. He hated being taken advantage of, especially by somebody he had done so much for. He also felt guilty about how he believed everything Sophia had said about Salman. He decided to call Sweeney. He let her know that he now had reason to believe that the victim was not completely honest. He also told her that he would be willing to help in Salman's early release.

She thanked him and appreciated his coming forward with the information.

With both attorneys using all the legal maneuvering together, they got Salman released three and a half years ahead of his six-year term.

***

Joseph went to meet with Salman after his release. He had lost a lot of weight. His business was being run by his son in his absence. Jose was still there. Salman was reflective, he always liked Joseph. *"I am glad you are doing well Joseph, I have looked at the books. I noticed you are all caught up with your rent. That's good. How's Danny and Selma?"*

"Everything's good. I just wanted to apologize to you on my family's behalf. You have always been good to us, but as far as my crazy sister-in-law is concerned, I had no control over her."

"That's okay Joseph, you are a good man. Because of you, I can't ask your family to leave my property. I went through so much suffering unnecessarily, but still when I look at you, I don't want to take any action against you."

"Thank you, Mr. Salman."

"Do you know what your crazy sister-in-law is up to these days?"

"She is living with that lawyer Foster, as far as I know."

"I don't think so. My attorney Sweeney told me Foster got cheated on. He kicked her out of his house. I guess your wife is hiding stuff from you."

"Oh my God! Really? I had no clue. Selma hides everything from me when it comes to her sister. I can't believe it. Big news like this and she keeps me in the dark. I wonder where she is living now. I really don't care, as long as she stays away from us."

"Well, I know Selma's type. She will do anything for her sister. Lie, cheat even kill somebody if she has to. Look at how

she turned on us. She is now a totally different person, than how we knew her. Unbelievable."

"I must agree. She will do anything. She is just blind when it comes to her sister."

"Well Joseph, I consider you a friend, you took my side against all odds. I don't forget my friends but I don't forget my enemies either."

Joseph was a little confused, wondering what he meant by that, but he didn't say anything.

When Joseph got home, he was too tired to have a fight with Selma. Besides he had given up on Selma to look at things realistically. She always had, and always would, take her sister's side no matter what. Still he calmly asked if what Salman had said was true. Selma confirmed it.

"I didn't tell you because I knew you would say derogatory things about her, and it's not easy for me to hear."

"Even if they are true?"

"Yes, even if they are true. I just can't take it. It's hard for me to explain why. Maybe because it's the blood relationship."

"I am trying to understand."

"Don't. Because you won't understand. So why bother?"

"So where is she living now?"

"Well that's another thing I didn't tell you, because I didn't want to hear your taunts and lectures. Remember when we went to the SCO party?"

"What's an SCO"?

"Syrian Christian Organization. So anyway, Sophia met a Lebanese guy, Tony, over there. They both liked each other. Foster found out. He asked her to leave his house, so she moved in with Tony."

"Just like that? Where are her morals? Didn't she feel any guilt, any remorse? Foster had done so much for her."

"There you go again. I knew you would start that again. That's why I don't tell you anything. You start making judgments.

She was not his wife. She can meet and be friends with anyone she wants. This is America."

"Really? Not too long ago, who got her out of that hellhole called Syria?"

"He did his job, and he got paid for it."

"Really, no use arguing with you."

"Don't then. I am going to sleep."

"Okay, go to sleep. I don't care. She can go to hell, as long as she stays away from me."

17

Another five months went by. Sophia was getting a little antsy about the security of her relationship with Tony. Everything was perfect. She wanted to get a little assurance that nothing would change, but Tony never showed any interest. Forget about marriage, even the talk of engagement was something he avoided, or quickly changed the subject whenever she brought it up.

She particularly felt lonely on the days he was not working from home. One such day, he had to report to work, he was running late and while in a rush, he forgot his cell phone in the bathroom. As soon as he stepped out the door, the phone rang. She didn't pick up to answer, but she quickly jotted down the number and hid it. She knew that he would be back any minute, as soon as he realized that his phone was missing. Sure enough, he came back, picked up his phone, mumbling some cuss words about being forgetful, and left.

When he left, she began to think certain things that she never thought about before. He was so particular about having his phone right next to him all the time. His excuse was that since he worked from home that was a privilege given to him by his employer. In return, for that privilege, he had agreed to be available by phone 24/7. When she first heard that explanation, it sounded logical to her. Another thing she noticed was that whenever the phone rang, he always took the call in privacy. There was a reason given for that too. *"In software engineering everything is so precise, I have to really focus on every little detail being said therefore I can't have any distractions."* That was logical also. On top of all that, she always wanted to give him the impression that she was easy going, non-argumentative, trusting. Now after having come to the sudden realization about all these things put together, it gave her cause for suspicion.

She was really scared. She pulled out the number she had hidden. Her hands were trembling and she was praying that it would be his work number. But unfortunately that wasn't the case.

A woman answered the phone. *"Hello, who's this"?*

"My name is Sophia. I am calling from California. Do you know Tony Cruz?"

"Yes, he is my husband. How do you know him?"

Sophia got such a jolt when she heard that, she stumbled and almost fell down, her phone fell from her hand. She could hear, *"Hello? Hello? Hello?"* in the distance coming from the phone on the floor. She didn't have the strength to pick it up. She sat down on the floor against the wall, staring in to blank space, the fallen phone a few feet away. Her perfect world was crumbling right in front of her eyes. AGAIN. Her Prince Charming was not what she thought he was. It was a bright sunny day, but everything looked dark. She felt like her head was going to explode with all the worrying thoughts rushing towards her all at-once. Suddenly she got the courage to find out more from that woman. She dialed the number again.

"I am sorry something happened and we got disconnected earlier."

"That's okay, what can I do for you? I am guessing you also got involved with Tony, and somehow got my number, and now you want to know about me? Am I right so far?"

"Yes, I have been living with him for the past seven months."

"That snake, no wonder. Look Miss, do yourself a favor. Don't fall into his fake charm and smooth talk. I have three kids with him and I am not the only woman he is involved with. I live in Boston. The other woman lives in Arizona and he has a child with her too. I guess he likes to spread his seeds all over. We are not divorced, we are separated. He keeps promising we will get back together."

Sophia had been hit hard many times in her life, and she always bounced back. She wasn't sure about this new one.

She felt severe dizziness and her head was pounding. She took a couple of sleeping pills, went to bed and lay down quietly. Before she knew it, it was three o'clock in the afternoon. It had been almost six hours since she had gotten the news. She was hoping it was a bad dream, but it wasn't.

For some strange reason, she decided to call Foster.

"John, can I talk to you for two minutes?"

"What is it? I am busy. What do you want?"

"I just wanted to let you know I am moving in with my sister."

"So, why are you telling me this? What do I care where you live or die? I have nothing to do with you anymore."

"Will you ever forgive me?"

"Why are you moving anyway, did you cheat on the lover boy too?"

Sophia started to cry. *"You are so mean."*

"Your crying is not going to have any effect on me anymore. I have seen that movie before. I will never forgive you for what you did. I don't like being stabbed in my back."

She hung up on him. She was sorry that she even called him.

She was reluctant to call her sister, because she knew how sad this would make her, and the hurt it would bring to her, but she had to. She didn't have a choice; her sister was her only ally.

"Selma, you are the sister of the unluckiest person in the entire world," she said with heavy sobs.

"Oh no, what happened this time"?

"I will never trust another man again in my life. I gave up everything for this man, and guess what I got in return? Somebody else's lying, cheating husband with four kids." She kept sobbing.

"Oh my poor baby. Please don't cry. Everything will be all right sweetheart, I promise you. Where are you? Do you want me to come over?"

"I am still at his place, but I can't stand it. He is at work right now. I really don't want to see his face again." Then Sophia proceeded to tell Selma how she had accidentally found out.

"Oh Sophia, don't worry. I know it must be hard. But remember you are tough as nails. You have handled even tougher situations before."

"Selma, I don't know what to do. I don't want to be here even for a day, but I don't know where will I go. I have no money, no car, no job, nothing. I just called Foster. He said he hates me."

"Sophia, you can come back here and live with me. I know we will have a problem with Joseph, but I will handle him."

"Selma I would never want you to jeopardize your marriage for my sake. You have already done so much."

"You are my sister, my blood, I will never abandon you. Joseph will be my problem not yours. Don't worry. When you are ready to move let me know."

When Tony came home, he immediately noticed the absence of any greeting from Sophia and her red eyes. *"What's wrong sweetie, something happen?"*

"Yes, something happened. I talked to your wife in Boston, that's what happened."

Tony was stunned. *"What?"* How? When? I mean I was going tell you everything," he stammered in desperation.

"Well, it's too late. She told me what I needed to know. You have three kids with her, and one from another woman in Arizona."

"Yes, but let me explain."

"There is nothing to explain, you had plenty of chances to explain in the last eight months."

"Sophia, please don't do this. You must let me tell you my side. You owe me that much. You just heard her side, it's not fair."

"It's not going to make any difference, but go ahead, I am listening."

"Okay, Kathy and I were fifteen and sixteen years old when we got married. We were kids. It was puppy love. We didn't know what we were doing. We were in high school together. Then she got pregnant and we didn't divorce because of the kids. The Arizona thing was a one-night affair. I went for a seminar in Phoenix one time, I met her there, and we both got drunk. She is a strict Catholic and wouldn't abort the child once she found out she was pregnant."

"Kathy said you keep promising her that you two will get back together."

"That was before I met you."

Sophia was not satisfied in the least. Her dreams had been shattered by this man for whom she had given up so much. He was the man she had loved with every fiber in her body. No other man had even come close. It was all gone, forever, never to come back.

"Tony, I want to move back with my sister."

"Sophia, please don't do this. We have such a good thing going. I will get a divorce, I promise."

"Tony, do whatever you want. You have broken something that is not fixable. I will never be able to get those feelings back."

"Sophia I am really sorry I disappointed you. I wish you would think again. You told me you didn't like living there, and you don't get along with your brother-in-law."

"It's all true, but I don't have a choice. I have made up my mind. I will never be able to trust you again and you cannot love someone you don't trust."

***

When Joseph came home from work, Selma had already conditioned herself for a huge argument with him. After dinner, when her son Danny went to his room, she told Joseph she had something important to discuss with him.

"What is it? I don't like the sound of it, are you ok?"

"It's about Sophia."

"What about Sophia? Haven't we discussed her enough times? What is it this time?"

"Well she found out some things about Tony that she didn't expect."

"Really? Usually people try to find out things about a person before they move in with them. Your sister does it the other way around. Anyways, what has that got to do with me? I gave up on her long time ago."

"Well, you may have given up on her, but I haven't. She is still my sister, and always will be."

"Okay, okay, so why are you bringing all this up? What's your point?"

"The things that she found out about Tony were so devastating for her that she doesn't want to live with him anymore."

"What did she find out? That he is murderer, terrorist, what?"

"That he has a wife and three kids. He is also involved with another woman who also has a kid."

"That's too bad. I am sorry, but I don't have any sympathy for her anymore. After what she did to Salman, it's just not possible for her to get on my good side."

"I know you don't have any sympathy for her, but don't forget she is my sister and therefore you won't be able to totally wash off your hands. Let me give it to you straight. She wants to get away from Tony, and she has nowhere to go. So I have asked her to move in with me."

"What? What did you say? Here? No way. That is not going to happen. Since when have you started making decisions on your own without checking with me?"

"Well, this is my house too, isn't it? I am not going to abandon her at the time of her need."

"Haven't we done enough for her? How many times are we going to bail her out? I haven't come across anybody who gets into more trouble than her."

135

"Have you known anyone who has gone through more tragedies than her?"

"You will still need to get Salman's permission for an extra person to live here, and I don't think you will get it this time."

"He won't give me the permission, but I am sure he will give it to you."

"Are you out of your mind? You expect me to go to him and say what? Oh Mr. Salman, remember that woman who falsely accused you of rape, for which you had spent three years in jail? The one who messed up your life, and your family's life? Can you please let her live in your property, free of charge? Is that what you expect me to do?"

"Look Joseph, this is something very important to me. I am not going to leave my sister in the lurch under any circumstances. You have to decide whether you are with me or against me on this. I'm not going to compromise when it comes to my family's well-being."

"What are you saying, you will leave me for her, if I don't agree?" Joseph couldn't believe his ears.

"Yes." Selma was firm.

"What about Danny? You will leave him too?"

"This has nothing to do with Danny. He is a grown man. He can decide on his own whether he wants to be with his mom or dad or both."

"I can't believe how this one woman can be such a destructive force, wrecking so many lives along the way and her sister keeps enabling her."

Joseph went and talked to Salman the next day. He was just as surprised as Joseph, when he first heard about Sophia's new shenanigans. He repeated to Joseph what he had said before. "Joseph, you are my friend. I don't like both sisters, but as long as you want to live there, I won't evict you. I hate your sister-in-law and won't forgive her for what she did to me and my family."

"I understand how you feel Mr. Salman, I hate her too. She is hell-bent on destroying my thirty-year marriage. I wish she was dead."

Sophia called Selma three days later to let her know that she was ready to move. Selma made arrangements with a moving company and everything got squared away fairly quickly. Sophia was back. Selma had already emptied her old room and had explained everything to Danny. Danny had always liked his auntie and didn't get himself involved in his parent's arguments about who was right and wrong.

Joseph was not on speaking terms with Sophia in spite of living in the same house. Tension had grown to a new level between Joseph and Selma since Sophia had moved in, but they always tried to be cordial when Danny was around.

Sophia was quite familiar with her old neighborhood and she liked going for walks around the block sometimes, to clear her mind and get some fresh air. One day, out of the blue she asked Selma where the nearest train station was. The reason she gave was a thought that crossed her mind, having never been on a train, since coming to America.

18

Sophia went for her familiar walk one afternoon and Selma noticed that she didn't come to the kitchen, as she usually did. It had become a routine for Sophia to go to the kitchen after the walks and make some fresh tea. Selma was doing her usual cooking in the kitchen, she looked at the clock, and it was close to four in the afternoon. She became curious and went to check Sophia's bedroom to see if she had decided to take an afternoon nap. She wasn't there. She called her on her cell phone. Her phone was turned off. That was highly unusual, she always had it powered on. Now what? She started panicking. She called the store, Danny picked up and told her Joseph had gone to pick up some stuff for the store. She called Joseph on his cell phone, it was off. Not knowing what to do next, she called the police station, they told her they wouldn't do anything unless the person was missing for twenty-four hours. She kept calling the store. Danny kept assuring her that he would have Joseph call her as soon as he came back.

Joseph called after an hour. He told her his phone was dead.

"What are we going to do Joseph? I am going out of my mind. She's been gone for four hours. She always lets me know where she is going. She went for a walk around one. She should have been back by one-thirty or two at the latest. It's now after five. Her phone is off, which never happens."

"I don't know what to tell you Selma. But I have to go back to work. Bye."

Minutes turned into hours for Selma, there was no sign of Sophia. Selma had Tony's number, he didn't know anything. Selma got Joseph to call Foster, who didn't know anything either.

Police were called again the next day. They promised an investigation.

19

Six months had gone by, and Sophia was still missing. Selma missed her terribly and worried every day. She wondered what could possibly have happened to her beautiful sister. There was rarely a day that went by when Selma didn't replay the events of the last two years to try and figure out where Sophia could be or, who could possibly have harmed her. She didn't want to believe the last scenario but her sister always called her. If she was unharmed, she would have called. Selma was completely sure of this. By the same token, she preferred to believe that Sophia just needed time, believing anything else would mean that she had come into foul play. Selma was not ready to accept this.

Sophia's life had been terribly tragic in the last five years. She had first lost her beloved husband to a terrorist bomb, and two years ago, her daughter Mona, the reason for her existence, had been taken by yet another terrorist bomb in Syria. She had come to the U.S. to start a new life. Selma had so wanted her to be happy here with her, and for a while she had been. There were so many things that had gone wrong and Sophia had made life-long enemies.

The first of those enemies was Salman. Sophia had accused him of rape and had him sent to jail after a brief trial. Salman's life had been ruined along with his reputation. He served three years of a six-year sentence after Sophia's lawyer worked with Salman's lawyer to have him released early. When he was released he made it no secret that he would never forgive her for what she had done to him. Could Salman have wanted revenge badly enough to kill Sophia? Selma knew he could be a harsh man.

Salman had been released early because Mr. Foster, Sophia's lawyer, had become convinced that she had somehow manipulated him into believing she had been raped. His change of heart came after he had become romantically involved with her and after two years, she had cheated on him. When Foster confronted Sophia about her affair, she had initially lied to him, which incensed him all the more. Foster was well connected. Could he have used his connections to bring harm to Sophia? It certainly wouldn't be the first time in history that a spurned lover killed. Selma wondered if it was motive enough for Foster.

Sophia had left Foster for Tony. Sadly, Tony had not been honest with Sophia and she discovered this when she spoke with his wife. When she confronted Tony, he didn't deny that he was married but had promised to divorce his wife explaining that they had been young when they were married and he wanted to spend his life with Sophia. Sophia had lost all faith and trust in him. She packed her bags and returned to Selma. Selma knew that Tony had been very hurt by Sophia for not giving him a second chance. Could he have been so dejected as to think that if he couldn't have her, no one else could? Did he make sure of this by kidnapping her? Killing her?

The enemy that hurt Selma the most was her own husband. He had never cared for Sophia and had made that clear from the beginning. He had only allowed Sophia to stay in his house for her, his wife of almost thirty years. Joseph had been embarrassed by Sophia's accusations of Salman who had always been more than kind and generous to his family. He had actually testified against Sophia at Salman's trial. Foster had been their attorney and had been instrumental in securing not only visas for Selma, Joseph, and their son, he had also managed to expedite the process for Sophia. After Sophia had cheated on him, Foster had no longer wanted anything to do with Joseph or his family. Joseph felt he had lost not only an attorney but a friend.

Selma knew that while Joseph had been angry about Salman and Foster, what had made him the angriest was when Sophia had left Tony, and was back in his house. Selma had invited her to live with them again. Joseph had been absolutely against it but Selma had given him an ultimatum, Sophia comes to live with them or she would leave him. Of course he had little choice except to acquiesce. Had it made him angry enough to want to hurt her? Kill her? Had he conspired with Salman?

There was always the possibility that Sophia had taken her own life. This was difficult for Selma to believe. Sophia hadn't seemed depressed. In fact, she seemed to be getting her life in order. She wanted to go back to school to get her law degree here in the U.S., she went for walks, and she was very much a part of Selma's life.

The last possibility was that Sophia had asked about the trains and where they went. Perhaps she had just decided to take a train and start over completely anew somewhere else. She hadn't taken a suitcase, personal belongings, even toiletries. But those things could be easily purchased wherever she was going. She did still have more than half of the money her late husband had arranged for her should anything happen to him.

Selma hoped against all hopes that Sophia had taken the train.

Reference

Alex: Dr. Alex Delgado, Sophia's late husband.

Andrew: Sophia's brother-in-law. Alex's brother.

David: Sophia's nephew. Selma's son.

Debbie: Sophia's lawyer/boyfriend's daughter.

Deena: Sophia's brother-in-law Andrew's daughter.

Dolly: Sophia's brother-in-law Andrew's wife.

Foster: John Foster, Sophia's lawyer/boyfriend.

Jose: Jose Lopez, manager where Sophia works.

Joseph: Joseph Mendes. Sophia's brother-in-law, Selma's husband.

Michael: Sophia's lawyer/boyfriend's son.

Mona: Sophia's late daughter.

Nancy: Nancy Sweeney, Salman's lawyer.

Rashid: Salman's son.

Razia: Salman's daughter.

Salman: Sophia's boss. Selma and Joseph's landlord.

Selma: Sophia's sister. Joseph's wife.

Tony: Tony Cruz, Sophia's middle-eastern boyfriend.

Zainub: Salman's wife.

Printed in the United States
By Bookmasters